SEP 0 5 2019

D0161004

Springdale Public Library
405 S. Pleasant
Springdale, AR 72764

DEC 0 3 2018

Eli's Triumph

Also from Joanna Wylde

Reaper's Property
Reaper's Legacy
Devil's Game
Silver Bastard
Reaper's Fall
Reaper's Fire
Reapers and Bastards
Shade's Lady
Rome's Chance

Eli's Triumph
A Reapers MC Novella
By Joanna Wylde

1001 Dark Nights

EVIL EYE
CONCEPTS

Springdale Public Library
405 S. Pleasant
Springdale, AR 72764

Eli's Triumph
A Reapers MC Novella
By Joanna Wylde

1001 Dark Nights

Copyright 2019 Joanna Wylde
ISBN: 978-1-970077-22-3

Foreword: Copyright 2014 M. J. Rose

Published by Evil Eye Concepts, Incorporated

All rights reserved. No part of this book may be reproduced, scanned, or distributed in any printed or electronic form without permission. Please do not participate in or encourage piracy of copyrighted materials in violation of the author's rights.

This is a work of fiction. Names, places, characters and incidents are the product of the author's imagination and are fictitious. Any resemblance to actual persons, living or dead, events or establishments is solely coincidental.

Dedication

For Liz Berry, Rebecca Zanetti, Margarita Coale, and Tina Gephart.

Acknowledgments from the Author

I'd like to thank Liz Berry and M.J. Rose for including me in 1001 Dark Nights, and for the grace and kindness they offered me during one of the most difficult years of my life. I'd also like to thank Kasi Alexander, Chelle Olson, Dylan Stockton and Kim Guidroz for the time and effort they put into producing this book. To say they went above and beyond is an understatement. It is appreciated.

Sign up for the 1001 Dark Nights Newsletter
and be entered to win a Tiffany Key necklace.

There's a contest every month!

Go to www.1001DarkNights.com to subscribe.

**As a bonus, all subscribers can download
FIVE FREE exclusive books!**

One Thousand and One Dark Nights

Once upon a time, in the future…

*I was a student fascinated with stories and learning.
I studied philosophy, poetry, history, the occult, and
the art and science of love and magic. I had a vast
library at my father's home and collected thousands
of volumes of fantastic tales.*

*I learned all about ancient races and bygone
times. About myths and legends and dreams of all
people through the millennium. And the more I read
the stronger my imagination grew until I discovered
that I was able to travel into the stories... to actually
become part of them.*

*I wish I could say that I listened to my teacher
and respected my gift, as I ought to have. If I had, I
would not be telling you this tale now.
But I was foolhardy and confused, showing off
with bravery.*

*One afternoon, curious about the myth of the
Arabian Nights, I traveled back to ancient Persia to
see for myself if it was true that every day Shahryar
(Persian: شهریار, "king") married a new virgin, and then
sent yesterday's wife to be beheaded. It was written
and I had read, that by the time he met Scheherazade,
the vizier's daughter, he'd killed one thousand
women.*

Something went wrong with my efforts. I arrived in the midst of the story and somehow exchanged places with Scheherazade – a phenomena that had never occurred before and that still to this day, I cannot explain.

Now I am trapped in that ancient past. I have taken on Scheherazade's life and the only way I can protect myself and stay alive is to do what she did to protect herself and stay alive.

Every night the King calls for me and listens as I spin tales. And when the evening ends and dawn breaks, I stop at a point that leaves him breathless and yearning for more. And so the King spares my life for one more day, so that he might hear the rest of my dark tale.

As soon as I finish a story... I begin a new one... like the one that you, dear reader, have before you now.

Prologue

~Peaches~

"Do you really think he can get away with it?" I asked, glancing toward Lemur. "I mean, I know he's evil enough…but I don't think Gus would let him, would he?"

The grubby little stuffed animal stared back at me, glass eyes cracked from hitting the floor too many times. His pink teacup sat on its saucer, untouched. He didn't say anything out loud, but I saw the answer in his face.

He didn't trust Eli King.

Neither did Eden, the doll sitting next to Lemur. She hadn't touched her tea, either, and who could blame her? Everything had been wrong since Eli moved in with us. Even our imaginary tea tasted wrong. Now it was nothing but water, and my special cakes were only chunks of bread.

My eyes slid toward the fourth place setting, set carefully on the old bandanna. The blue cup. That's where Gus was supposed to sit. It should be me, Lemur, Eden, and Gus.

Always.

But Gus was too busy to play with us today. He was working on his motorcycle, and he'd asked stupid Eli to help him. Sliding on my butt across the porch's battered boards, I peered through the railing to study the two of them.

They crouched in the driveway next to the bike—my giant, grumpy, snuggly Gus and a stinky boy who liked to think he was so much older than me, but he wasn't. Eli was only seven, and they were making him do first grade over again. Maybe he'd flunk this year, too. Then we'd be in the same class.

Gus poked at the engine with one of his tools. I couldn't see what kind because Eli was between me and him, which was pretty much where he always was.

Between me and Gus.

And if Lemur was right, Eli was doing it on purpose. Eden agreed… Sometimes, Lemur was wrong, but Eden? Eden was almost always right, and the two of them together had never been wrong before. There was only enough space for one kid in this house, and Eli was ruthless.

He'd already taken over half my bedroom.

My eyes narrowed as I considered his messy brown hair, hanging too long across the back of his neck. Maybe I could Superglue it to the bed while he was sleeping.

"Eli, go grab me a beer," Gus said, his deep voice rumbling across the yard. His bike rumbled like that, too. It needed a tune-up because the motorcycle club was doing something *very important* later this week.

Fixing the bike was worth canceling the tea party. I was okay with that. But when Gus needed a helper, he should've called me. I was the one who should be running toward the kitchen door to fetch a bottle.

"I've got to get rid of him," I whispered softly, trying to think of something. There had to be a way to make Eli go away. "I wonder if he's scared of spiders?"

My toys didn't answer. Turning around, I looked at them, biting my lip. I could tell that Lemur had an idea, but Eden seemed to be shaking her head at me. Her eyes had opened wider than usual, and I realized she was afraid.

She thought Eli might hurt her and Lemur.

My tummy flipped, and I felt sick.

I could see why Eden was afraid. Eli had already broken one of my teacups, and nobody but me knew that Eden and Lemur weren't just toys. They were *alive*. Not only living, but the best friends a girl could ever have.

Suddenly, this wasn't just about my room.

This was about protecting my best friends.

"Don't worry, I'll hide you," I told them, swallowing hard. "Before I do anything else, I'll hide you. And then I'll go find some spiders and put them in his bed. Or maybe a snake. I'll keep us safe from him. No matter what it takes, I'll get rid of Eli King. I promise."

Chapter One

Starkwood Saloon
Washington State
Present day

~Peaches~

"What do you think those bikers are talking about?" Megan asked, leaning next to me against the railing.

"Which ones?" I said, locking eyes with a man sitting across the room.

Eli King.

The only guy on Earth with the power to drive me absolutely crazy just by existing. Not the good kind of crazy, either. More of a plotting-vengeance-at-four-in-the-morning-because-you-can't-unhear-him-fucking-his-girlfriend-through-a-wall kind of crazy.

My nemesis sat enjoying a beer with three of the five Reapers who'd sauntered into the bar thirty minutes earlier. They'd taken over one of the far tables, settling in for the duration while the other two disappeared into the back with Gus.

Eli had abandoned his post to join them—apparently, club membership came before his job, which shouldn't have surprised me. His uncle always put the club first, too. That annoyed me, but what'd annoyed me more was the way Eli had asked for a beer when I took their order. Like I was his serving wench, and he wasn't the damned bartender who was supposed to be pouring those beers instead of drinking them.

Now, he leaned back in his chair, all relaxed and smug. Watching me.

Probably pretending he was a king for real. *Maybe I should start a rumor that he needs to wear a plastic crown to get it up…*

Eli cocked a brow as I narrowed my eyes. Then he raised his bottle in salute as if to say, "*Hey, Peaches, having fun working while I sit on my ass drinking?*"

God, I loathed him. I hated his stupid long legs and his dumb arm muscles, and his hair. He'd gotten it cut, I realized. Had to have been that morning because it'd still been all shaggy last night. Definitely hadn't shaved, though. Just a hint of stubble around his chin… *Shit.*

Eli was being all sexy today, and that was the worst.

He lifted his bottle, flicking his tongue across his bottom lip right before taking a sip. I found my breath faltering because it reminded me of—

No. Not going there. *Never* going there. Didn't matter how attractive he was, didn't matter that Gus said he'd always seen us together. And it *really* didn't matter that Eli's ass looked absolutely fucking fantastic in a pair of faded jeans.

The man was a force of pure destruction, something I knew all too well, and the fact that he'd come back from prison even more pumped up and ripped than before, well…that was just God's sick joke on women everywhere. Under all those muscles, Eli was still the asshole who'd taken Lemur hostage when I was five.

The torment hadn't stopped there, either.

When I was sixteen, he'd beaten up my first boyfriend, Mark McDougal. Mark had dumped me after that. Said I wasn't worth getting an ass-kicking. Not even when I wore my black bikini. Just thinking about it made my jaw clench. *Ugh.*

I forced myself to take a nice, deep, refreshing yoga breath, repeating a peaceful mantra as I refused to notice how Eli's throat moved when he swallowed.

Inhale the goodness and love. Exhale the negativity and darkness.

He lowered the beer, still holding my eyes. Crap. He'd gotten into my head again, and he knew it. Not only that, he knew that I knew, which meant we weren't just catching each other's gaze across the room by accident. Nope. This was now the latest battle in our little war. My fingers tightened around the lemon I'd been slicing, sending juice squirting across the counter.

Yet another mess I'd have to clean up because of Gus's stupid nephew.

"The two guys in the office with Gus," Megan said, breaking through my thoughts. I hadn't even remembered she was standing next to me, let alone what we'd been talking about.

"What?" I asked, trying not to blink because Eli wasn't blinking.

"What do you think they're talking about?"

"Doesn't matter. You shouldn't be curious about them," I replied absently, my eyes starting to burn.

"Are you serious?" she asked, a hint of laughter in her voice. "That sounds a little dramatic."

I sighed. Megan had only been waiting tables at the Starkwood Saloon for a week. She didn't know the rules yet, so I'd have to educate her.

"They're part of the Reapers Motorcycle Club," I said. "And it's not a great idea to be asking questions about them. Doesn't matter what they're talking about because it's none of our business... Hey, does it seem like he's planning something to you? I don't trust that look on his face. That's the look he gets when he's up to something."

"Huh?"

"Eli," I said shortly. My eyes were seriously starting to hurt. Why wasn't he blinking? Was he even human? *Maybe he's half demon. Demons probably don't have to blink at all.*

"Eli?" she asked, sounding confused. "Why are we talking about Eli?"

"He's been watching me."

"Um, I think he's just drinking a beer," Megan said. "Maybe checking out your boobs a little, but that's nothing new."

Hmm... It couldn't possibly be that simple, but it did give me an idea. Maybe it was time to create a diversion. I shifted my shoulders, expanding my chest.

Disappointingly, his eyes stayed on mine.

"Someday I'm gonna own this bar, and firing his ass is the first thing I'll do."

Megan giggled. "That sounded sort of super-villain-ish. Do you have a lair? I wish I had a lair..."

I blinked, caught off guard. I hadn't realized that I'd said the words out loud. Eli smirked at me, gloating because he'd just won our little pissing contest. *Dammit!*

"I can't believe I wrote to him in prison," I told her, turning my back on the bikers. "Never should've been nice to him. He probably thinks that, deep down inside, we're friends or something. We're never going to be friends."

"Didn't he give you a ride home after work last night?" she asked, her voice light.

"Gus made him," I snapped.

"And did Gus make him hug you the other day?"

"He caught me and gave me a noogie. And it hurt, too. It's not a hug if it leaves bruises."

"He left bruises?" Megan asked, startled. *Shit*. I might be able to justify a rumor about him not being able to get it up, but telling her that he'd hurt me for real…yeah, that probably crossed a line.

"No," I admitted. "That was an exaggeration. But he's still pure evil, so don't fall for his shit. Or sleep with him. Every time a waitress sleeps with him, she ends up quitting without notice. Then I have to cover their shifts."

Megan nodded, looking a little uncomfortable. "Okay, then… Um, I think I'll go check the bathrooms. Make sure there's no ugly surprises before things start getting busy."

"Great idea," I told her, and she scuttled off. Then I reached for a washcloth because I had lemon juice to clean up. Then I'd have to go back over there and check on them. See if they wanted more… Eli would, I could already tell. Not because he was big on drinking, though.

He just wouldn't be able to resist an opportunity to order me around.

* * * *

~Eli~

"Looks like you gentlemen could use another round," Peaches said, her voice so sweet it hurt my teeth. She offered bright smiles to the brothers around the table. No smile for me, though.

Kinda surprising, actually.

Usually, the more pissed off she was, the sweeter her smiles got. Sweet and polite and so damned terrifying that I'd been afraid to sleep in the same room as her after Gus took me in. I liked to think that was because of the snakes she kept putting in my bed, but they weren't the only reason. Nope. The scariest part had been the way she'd glare at me through the darkness every night.

I spent a lot of time that first year wondering if Peaches would be strong enough to smother me with a pillow. You know, if I fell asleep before she did. Which never happened. Not once. Because I really didn't want to find out the answer.

At least I'd always held my own with the payback.

It'd probably been for the best when her mom and Gus broke up, all things considered. We might've killed each other for real if she hadn't moved out after second grade.

"I'd love another beer, gorgeous," Rollins said. He'd been the Bellingham sergeant-at-arms for more than a decade, and the man was one scary-ass motherfucker. But Peaches didn't seem too worried.

The girl had no sense of self-preservation.

I'd seen her go after a man my size with a bat during a bar fight just last month. It was shit like this that'd bothered me the most when I was locked up…knowing she was out in the world, unprotected, and there wasn't a damned thing I could do about it.

And Peaches needed protecting, no question. Instead of backing away from Rollins like a sensible woman, she giggled, then *accidentally* brushed against him as she leaned over to pick up his empty bottle. The move essentially flashed her tits for all the world to see, and I felt my smile stiffen. Fuckin' hated it when she did that.

Peaches knew this. That's why she did it.

Rollins shot me a look, then very deliberately checked her out. Mostly to piss me off—because he was an asshole—but also because he was a guy with a dick. And it was hard to blame him for appreciating a sight like that. The girl had an amazing rack. One I'd spent no small amount of time thinking about over the years.

High school had been hell for me and Gus both, although the reasons were different.

Peaches had started popping out of her shirts the summer before ninth grade. I could still remember my uncle telling me we needed to have a talk that August. He'd grabbed us a couple of beers, and we'd found a shady spot out back. Then he'd explained that it was my job to protect her from all the guys who'd be trying to get into her pants once they saw those new tits.

He'd also told me what'd happen if I touched her myself, starting with a casual comment about how many bodies were hidden out in the forest lands.

Bodies nobody would ever find.

Keeping her safe from the boys at school had been easy. Keeping my own hands off her was the hard part. Wasn't the only hard part, either. Most days, I'd jacked off two or three times thinking about that girl.

"I'd be thrilled to fetch you another drink," Peaches cooed at Rollins, all sunshine and flowers. "And it's good to see you again. How's Bella doing? I sure enjoyed meeting her last year."

Rollins' face softened. A chill touched my spine—the same one I'd felt in the darkness when Peaches and I had shared a room all those years ago.

Guy like that shouldn't be so easy to manipulate, yet she'd just turned him from horny dick to whipped pussy with one question. "She's due any day now."

"I didn't know you had a baby on the way!" she squealed, and her eyes lit up. Jesus Christ, we were all fucked now. Peaches *loved* babies, and she never got tired of talking about them.

Some nights in prison, I'd have nightmares about another guy knocking her up. Other nights, I'd wake up shaking and covered in cold sweat because I'd flashed back to the time she'd suckered me into giving her a ride to a baby shower.

This was truly terrifying shit.

"I'm ready for another drink," I announced, cutting off the conversation before things got ugly.

Peaches turned on me, fury flashing in her eyes before she tamped it down. In an instant, her face was blank again. Still, it'd been enough to give away her new game.

She'd decided to give me the silent treatment.

"Draft this time," I added, wondering how long she'd be able to keep it up. Her smile reappeared, but I sensed the effort it took. Perfect. Time for another jab. "And try to pour it right so there's not too much head on it."

She stilled, her smile tightening. I could almost hear her arguing with herself. Would she stay quiet or go on the attack? Then her eyes narrowed.

Attack it was.

"Don't worry, I'd never give you head, Eli," she said sweetly. Rollins snorted, and I blew her a kiss. Goddamn, but I loved pissing her off.

"Hey, Eli!" Gus called out across the room, his raspy voice disrupting the moment. He sounded older every day. Old and tired.

"Looks like they're ready for you," Rollins drawled, his laughter fading.

"Yup," I agreed, keeping it casual. Couldn't be one hundred percent sure what was about to happen, but I could make an educated guess.

If that guess was right, I'd spent half my life waiting for this moment.

Pushing back my chair, I stood, pausing to survey the room. The Starkwood Saloon hadn't changed much over the years, at least not on the surface. Menu had gotten better while I was gone, though, and profits were up. That was all thanks to Peaches.

It'd be a shame to fire her, but I'd do it if she couldn't show some respect once I was her boss. Still, I'd rather have her working under me. Or just under me in general. I swallowed... Yeah, this was gonna get complicated.

Gus slapped my back when I reached him, although I couldn't tell anything from his expression. Following his gaze, I realized he was watching Peaches as she collected the empties. Then she started walking toward the bar with her hips swinging. That's when it hit me again—the same feeling that'd made me break that teacup and steal that stuffed animal of hers all those years ago.

Got me every single fuckin' time.

"Hey, Peaches," I said, well aware I was playing with fire. Gorgeous, glorious fire. Totally worth the burn. She pretended she hadn't heard me, but she was listening. Time to push more buttons. "You know, you'd be a lot prettier if you smiled."

She didn't respond, but I saw her fingers whiten around the empty bottles. Satisfaction rolled through me, and my cock twitched. Then I pictured her glaring at me right before I bent her over the bar. That gave my cock a lot more than a twitch.

Yeah. Firing her would suck… And now I was thinking about sucking…

You gotta shut this shit down, I told myself firmly, which was just stupid. Shutting it down wasn't an option. Peaches Taylor had crawled under my skin when I was seven years old, and by now, I was addicted to the sensation. Sooner or later, I'd bend her over that bar for real.

Until then, I'd just have to get off by torturing her.

Seemed only fair, all things considered. I was a strong man. I'd had to fight for my club, and then fight to protect myself in prison. There weren't a lot of things on Earth that scared me…but every time I saw a snake, my heart about pounded right out of my chest. That's how much those fuckers freaked me out.

Peaches still owed me for those fucking snakes.

Chapter Two

~Eli~

Gage nodded as I walked into the office, pushing a battered folding chair toward me with his foot. He sat in one just like it, looking relaxed. That was a good sign. Rance had settled in behind Gus's desk, his face thoughtful.

"So, you know why we're here, right?" asked Gage, getting straight to the point. The question might've felt like a trap coming from someone else. But he was the president of my chapter of the Reapers MC, and I'd trust him with my life. *Had* trusted him with my life, actually. More than once.

"I'm thinking it's about the bar," I said, glancing toward Gus. The old man nodded, and a tension I hadn't even realized I'd been carrying lifted.

"Gus says he's ready to retire, and we need someone we can trust running the place," Gage continued.

That was an understatement. The Starkwood wasn't just a bar. It was a meeting place on some nights and a convenient alibi on others. Not to mention handy as hell for taking in dirty money and spitting it back out again, all shiny and clean. My new part to play wasn't a surprise, either. Gus had always planned on me taking over someday. I'd planned on it, too—until I got sent to prison.

The club had done their part, bringing in the best lawyer their money could buy. He'd ultimately gotten me out of prison on appeal, but that'd come down to luck. For all we'd known, I could've been stuck in that cell for the next two decades.

That's why they'd needed a backup plan—Peaches.

I knew Gus had talked to her last year about buying him out, and she was gonna be *pissed* when she learned that I was taking her place. Again.

"I'll give you a good deal," Gus told me, clearing his throat. "But it has to be reasonable, or it'll look suspicious."

"The money is covered," I reminded him. "Haven't touched it since I got out."

"Obviously, the club will throw in some resources, too," Rance added. "Just be aware that if you do this, there's no going back."

Somehow, I managed not to laugh out loud at that one. Wasn't a good idea to laugh at a club president—not unless he was joking on purpose. "All due respect, I already served five years for the club. Running a bar is nothing compared to that."

"And we appreciate it," Gage said. "We all know what you did. You were tested, and you didn't fail. We'll get the papers drawn up. Thanks for coming over, Rance."

"Anytime," the Bellingham president grunted. "And, Eli, I wasn't trying to question your commitment. Gage is right. We all know what you did for us. You know you've always got our support if you need it."

"Appreciated," I told him, savoring the moment. This was mine, now. All mine. Savage triumph hit as the full reality started to sink in. Today, the Starkwood Saloon was finally mine. Sure, I'd be working in a partnership with the Reapers, but I'd never expected anything else. Hell, I'd grown up in the club.

We all stood and slapped backs like it was any other day. Then Gage and Rance stepped out, leaving Gus and me alone in the office. I looked around the grubby room. It still held the same battered desk that'd been there when I was a child, although the old couch had been replaced at some point.

First time I'd ever gotten laid was on that couch.

"You could've given me a heads-up," I said finally, after a long pause. Gus shrugged, and I noticed that his shoulders seemed narrower. Less bulky. My uncle was getting old.

"Wasn't a done deal until today. There's a process for things like this. Gotta follow protocol."

I considered that, realizing he was right. And we still had one more step in that protocol. Not an official move, but an important one. Shit. Just thinking about it was enough to kill my mood.

"So…you gonna give her the news or should I do it?"

Gus sighed heavily. "My decision, my job to tell her. But I'm not ashamed to admit that I'm nervous. She might just torch the place."

The point was valid.

"Yeah, we should probably hide the matches."

"Peaches won't need matches," Gus said slowly, raising a hand to rub his temple. "She'll shoot fire straight out of her eyes. Her mom could do it, too. Never piss off a Taylor woman, Eli. They'll make you pay for the rest of your life."

"Too late."

Gus grunted, then nodded. "Can't argue with that. Do me a favor. If she kills me, make sure they never figure out what happened. It should look like an accident, not a murder. Understand? She's the closest thing I've got to a daughter." He shook his head slowly. "You know, if you'd claimed her ass when you got out, this wouldn't be such a big fucking deal."

"Have you *met* Peaches?" I asked, raising a brow. "It needs to be her idea. Otherwise, it's not happening."

A faint, bittersweet smile spread across my uncle's face. "Yeah, you're right about that. Her mom was the same way... I fucked that shit up, and I've regretted it every day since. Don't make the same mistake, you got me? She'll never forgive you."

"Oh, I'm aware. She still hasn't forgiven me for locking her in that closet. I was only twelve, for fuck's sake."

"You left her in there overnight."

"At least there wasn't a snake in there."

"Tell yourself whatever you have to, son," he replied, shaking his head. "Now, I'd best get this over with. Send her in, will you? Oh, and I was serious about covering things up if she murders me."

"I know. I'll go round up some bleach and a tarp while you tell her the news."

* * * *

~Peaches~

"Excuse me?" I asked, the words sharp and precise.

Gus wore the same calm, steady expression he always wore. Normal. Like he hadn't just smashed my world to pieces with one sentence.

"You heard me, sweetheart."

"No..." I said slowly. "Because it *sounded* like you just told me that you're selling the bar to Eli. And that can't be right. Because *I'm* buying the bar. We talked about it two years ago, remember? We even ran the numbers. We're supposed to do a contract for deed at the end of the year. That's only six months from now, Gus."

"Eli has cash," he said flatly. "With you, I'd have to carry a contract. I'll be dead before you pay it off, baby. He made the offer, and I accepted. The deal is done."

"What?" I asked, stunned. "Eli has *cash?* That's crazy. He doesn't even have his own apartment! He doesn't have a job history—nothing. There's no way."

"His dad died while he was in prison," Gus replied.

"He's never even met the guy. You're the one who raised him."

"True," Gus said. "The man was shit, no question. But he got killed by a drunk driver, and the driver's insurance offered a settlement. Eli was the only heir. It came in a lump sum, and it's been sitting in the bank ever since. That's a much better deal for me than a contract for deed."

"But we had a *deal,*" I insisted. "Eli has no clue how to run this place. He's only been back a few months, and half the time, he's fucking off with your club brothers. He spent the whole afternoon drinking instead of working!"

"Peaches, honey—"

"Don't *honey* me, Gus," I snapped, a wave of fury welling up deep within my chest. "You *promised* me this place. Said you could count on me to run it right. Or did I hallucinate all those conversations?"

"I can count on Eli to run it right, too," Gus said, holding my gaze. Funny how he managed to keep eye contact. You'd think it'd be logistically impossible, what with the giant-ass knife he'd just stabbed into my back. "You're damned good at your job, Peaches. I'm proud of everything you've accomplished here. But Eli is my blood, and he's part of my club. I know you don't want to hear this, but the only reason I talked to you about taking over was because I thought he was gone. He was always my first choice. Even if it wasn't for the cash."

His words made me see red. Literally. Flashes of crimson danced at the edges of my vision, and the air in the room seemed too thick for me to inhale at all, let alone catch my breath.

Motherfucking Eli King had done it again.

First, he'd stolen half my bedroom.

Then he'd stolen Gus.

Now, he was stealing the Starkwood right out from under me, and I could tell from the expression on my boss's face that he'd been telling the truth—this really had been his plan all along. Turning away from Gus, I ran my fingers through my hair, trying to think. *How could he do this to me?*

I wanted to kill Gus. No. I wanted to kill *Eli.* I wanted to kill him dead and then stomp on his body and set it on fire. Because no matter what I did, it would never be enough.

Eli *always* won.

"I'd like a few minutes alone," I said, forcing my voice to stay steady and even, despite the fact that I could feel screams of rage fighting to escape. I heard the creak of Gus's chair as he stood, and the sound of his feet as he came to stand behind me. He probably had that look on his face—the same one he always wore when I was sad. Soft and kind, as if he wanted to wrap me in his arms and protect me and keep me safe forever.

I'd trusted that look when I was a little girl. Believed it when I was a teenager, too, even after I'd learned the truth about why my mom had left him. And I'd trusted it two years ago when he'd first talked to me about buying the bar.

God, I was such an idiot.

"Gus just wasn't the man I wanted him to be." My mom's words echoed through my head. *"My only mistake was thinking I could change him, Peaches."*

Why the hell hadn't I listened to her?

"Doesn't feel right, leaving you like this."

"I don't really care how you feel, Gus," I said, refusing to look at him. Instead, I fixed my gaze on the signed poster from Daytona Bike Week that I'd given him for Christmas a couple of years ago. Finding it hadn't been easy. I'd had to hunt down the artist, a guy who worked at Harley Davidson.

"I'll always be here for you, baby girl."

His voice held pain, and a part of me wanted to push down the anger. Wanted to wrap my arms around him and tell him it was okay. Just like I'd said it was okay when he canceled my tea party to work on his bike. Or all the times he'd asked me to help close the bar, even when I'd worked doubles all week. I'd never told him no. I loved him too much. Loved him and the fucking Starkwood.

My fury exploded, and I spun on him.

"Get out."

Gus took a step back, and his eyes widened. He seemed almost afraid. Good. He *should* be frightened, because he'd just fucked up. Fucked up big time. Things would never be the same between us again, because Mom had been right about him.

I'd be damned if I'd give him another chance to hurt me.

He opened his mouth, but I raised my hand, holding it in front of his face like a stop sign.

"Get *out!*" I said, my voice rising. "Get the fuck out of here, you lying bastard!"

I stepped forward into his space, backing him toward the hallway with the force of my raw anger. His feet had barely cleared the threshold before I slammed the door in his face. I slid home the oversized barrel bolt with a satisfying thud, then turned to look at the poster again.

Rip it down, the rage hissed. *Slice it to pieces. He doesn't deserve it.*

It was a solid idea, and I knew exactly how to do it, too. Stalking around the desk, I reached up and under the flat surface, fingers feeling for the survival knife Gus had kept hidden there for as long as I could remember. That would be in addition to the gun he'd taped up along the inner right side, and the baseball bat leaning against the battered file cabinet.

It only took a few seconds to find the knife, and one more to pop the snap holding it in the scabbard. The blade slipped free, ten inches of steel alloy that'd be more than enough to shred the pathetic reminder of how much of myself I'd given to Gus's bar.

No.

It was *Eli's* bar now.

I raised a finger to test the blade, mesmerized as a tiny bead of blood welled up from a cut so clean that I hardly registered the pain. The sight fed the rage burning deep within, and I thought about Eli's smug face as he taunted me.

"You know, you'd be a lot prettier if you smiled."

Oh, I could give him a smile. A truly lovely one. Right across his smug throat. Gus thought Eli should have the bar? Fine, Eli could have the fucking bar. Eli could have everything.

Good luck trying to enjoy it once I'm done with you, motherfucker.

Chapter Three

~Eli~

I prowled through the bar, unable to focus.

Gage, Rance, and the rest of my club brothers had cleared out by the time I left Gus's office. Apparently, their business here was done, and socializing wasn't on the agenda. Probably looking to avoid any drama.

Hard to blame them.

The night that Glory—Peaches' mom—had walked in on Gus fucking one of the waitresses in the storeroom was something of a club legend. To say that she'd raised hell was a bit of an understatement... Only luck had saved the Starkwood from burning down.

Hopefully, history wouldn't be repeating itself.

The thought carried me down the hallway, and I found myself outside the office door. It couldn't have been more than ten minutes since Peaches and Gus had started talking, but it felt like hours. Nervous energy filled my body, pulling me in fifty different directions at once. Part of me wanted to go tell the staff who was in charge now.

Stake my claim and make it official.

Another part wanted to celebrate. Maybe get drunk. Getting laid would probably do some good, too. At the same time, I wanted to go through the books, start wrapping my head around the totality of the business. Gus would help with the transition, of course, and I'd grown up watching him. I knew the basics. Still, there was a big difference between being the boss's nephew and being the boss.

Oh, and there'd be a metric fuck ton of legal paperwork to deal with, too.

Logistics. Money transfers.

Title companies were a thing, although I wasn't quite sure what they did. Would I need one of those?

I had no fucking clue about stuff like this. As of this morning, I'd owned a motorcycle, three towels, a laundry basket of clothes, my leathers, a helmet, and my club colors. Oh, and that stuffed animal. Going from that to owning property and a business would be a hell of an adjustment.

This was going to take time. Time and hard work.

Celebrating probably shouldn't be my highest priority.

Leaning back against the wall, I crossed my arms over my chest as I waited. There was a storm building in Gus's office. I could all but smell Peaches' anger and betrayal, and I actually felt a twinge of guilt.

No. Fuck that shit.

I'd earned this bar, paid for it with five long years in prison, holding my tongue and taking the punishment for a crime that wasn't mine. Gus owed me for that alone. The fact that he'd get a cash payout was just a bonus at this point.

No reason for me to feel guilty. And that was the truth.

Still, I could see how much this sucked for Peaches. She'd put in time, too. Time and good faith. Riling her up was a blast, but I'd never wanted her hurt. Not for real. I cared about the girl. Cared about her a lot.

Too much.

Gus had been weak. I loved my uncle, but he'd fucked this one up big time. She deserved better from him—and from me. I should be in there with them. Decision made, I reached for the door.

"Get *out!* Get the fuck out of here, you lying bastard!"

The door burst open, and Gus stumbled out, walking backward. I caught his arm and steadied him as the slab slammed shut again. I heard the heavy bolt sliding shut, locking us out. My uncle looked at me, then sighed.

"Actually went better than I expected."

"Glad I don't have to deal with hiding a body."

"Not yet," he replied, then sighed again. "She's not a happy camper. Probably should've warned her that our plans might change once you got out."

"Why didn't you? Would've been a lot easier on her."

"Guess I didn't want her turning on me," my uncle admitted, surprising me with his honesty. "I knew she'd hate me for it. God, but I miss her mom. Saw her in town a couple weeks ago. It's been twenty years, and Glory still won't even look at me."

Raw pain filled his eyes. I cleared my throat, uncomfortable. Fuck. I didn't like this. Didn't like my girl hurting, and didn't like having to see my uncle like this.

Didn't like knowing I was part of it.

A loud thump came from behind the door, breaking the moment. There was a crash, and then some kind of tearing noise. Shit.

Some women pouted when they got upset.

Others cried.

Peaches had always skipped that part, moving straight to revenge. Another crash. This one so hard that the door rattled. I pictured her all pissed off in there, those glorious tits of hers straining against the front of her low-cut black Starkwood Saloon shirt. My cock twitched. Christ, she was hot when she got angry.

Her cheeks would be flushed, and she'd run her fingers through that wild, dark hair of hers in frustration.

Total sex hair.

Now my dick was getting hard, thinking about grabbing onto the strands, pulling her head back while I fucked her from behind.

I am such an asshole. The only woman I really cared about—hell, probably loved on whatever level I was capable of feeling such things—had just lost her dream.

A decent guy wouldn't be turned on right now.

Unfortunately, my sense of decency had died in prison, leaving behind a man who got off on the idea of sparring with Peaches. The door shook again, followed by a wordless scream of rage.

"Maybe I should—?"

"No," I said, cutting Gus off. "I'll handle this. You go out to the bar. Cover damage control. I'll take care of Peaches."

"I know that look on your face, boy," he said, warning clear in his voice. "You don't get to—"

"All due respect, Gus, but we're not in high school anymore. This is my business, not yours."

My uncle's eyes widened, and for a moment, I thought he might challenge me. Then he looked away, nodding slowly.

"Guess you're right," he said.

Another crash rattled the door as he walked away, and I settled in to wait. Sooner or later, she'd run out of shit to break in there. I wasn't stupid enough to think that'd be enough to exhaust her rage, so I'd best be ready.

In the distance, I heard Gus's loud voice announcing that everyone needed to head outside for a break.

The door rattled again, then it burst open.

Peaches stepped out, and the first thing I saw was the way her eyes seemed to shoot pure fire.

Just like her mother's.

The second thing was the giant fucking survival knife gripped tightly in her right hand. A sane man might've taken that as a bad sign, but I'd left my sanity behind me, right next to my decency.

This wasn't a threat. This was an opportunity.

Someone had to take her down, and as her new boss, that definitely qualified as my job. Only responsible thing to do, really... Couldn't let the customers see her like this.

If I got lucky, I'd get to wrestle with her a bit in the process.

"Still think I'd be prettier if I smiled?" she asked, the words intense and full of hate.

"Yeah," I replied, licking my lips. A wave of heat surged down my spine, and I felt my hips shift restlessly as my cock throbbed. "But pretty is boring. I like you better when you're pissed off. Makes me want to push you down over that desk and fuck you."

* * * *

~Peaches~

"You always find a way to make it worse, don't you?" I asked, fingers tightening around the knife's grip.

Eli nodded, wearing the same sly, taunting smirk he'd worn when he'd held his BB gun to Lemur's head all those years ago.

"You sure you want it to go down like this?" he asked, eyes flicking toward the knife. "That's a very grown-up toy, and you're not a very big girl. Hardly big enough to hold it."

Fucking.

Bastard.

He wouldn't stop until I snapped, of course. He got off on poking at me, and I knew it...but for once, I didn't care. I'd stepped out of that office fully intending to slit his throat. This just confirmed the decision.

And once I finished with him? Well, then I'd go after Gus. Because fuck them. Fuck both of them and their stupid club.

Eli just stood there, gloating. Waiting for me to bitch him out? I didn't bother. Shifting my feet for balance, I lowered the knife between us, then took a steadying breath. The blade was heavy, but I was strong from years of hauling big serving trays over my head.

I lunged.

He reacted instantly—Eli had always been fast—his hand flashing out to catch my arm, jerking it high over my head as he stepped into my space. But this wasn't our first fight, or even our first fight with a knife. I'd nearly taken his eye out at a second-grade picnic. I *knew* how he moved, and I knew how to use it to my advantage. The knife was just the bait. I ignored the pain of his fingers squeezing my wrist and brought my knee up toward his crotch with every ounce of strength I possessed.

It was random luck that saved his balls. He chose that exact moment to twist my arm down and around. That sent me lurching to the side, my knee smashing into his thigh instead of his nuts. Eli's eyes narrowed, and the smirk disappeared.

Good. About time he remembered to take me seriously.

His grip on my wrist tightened, squeezing the bones together until they screamed in pain. I kept hold of the knife. He could break my wrist for all I cared.

Taking advantage of his distraction, I jabbed the fingers of my left hand toward the little hollow at the base of his throat. He managed to partially deflect that, too, loosening his grip on my knife hand in the process. I tried to jerk it free, my other hand dodging his as he tried to catch it. The man might be fast, but I was faster. Fast and determined.

This time, I went for his nipple.

I twisted it hard through his shirt, savoring the vivid red flush that came over his face. Eli's nipples were sensitive as hell, always had been. It'd been a go-to for me all through elementary school. I hadn't tried it since we were adults, but some things never changed.

Then he caught my wrist, wrenching my grip loose from the nipple in a move that must've been excruciating—I wouldn't let him go easily. That's where I had the advantage, I realized. Eli wouldn't hurt me. I knew it on some deep level. Instinctively.

He had both my hands now.

That should've been enough to stop me, but I was just getting started. I bucked against him, then threw my weight backward. He followed me, pushing me through the office door.

"Stop fighting," he grunted. I answered with a headbutt, which would've been a lot more effective if he wasn't so fucking tall. Instead of knocking him on his ass movie-style, I mostly whacked the hell out of my forehead on his chin. "Jesus, Peaches. You're gonna hurt yourself."

I tried to knee him again. He blocked it with his leg, using my arms to push me away just enough to transfer my wrists to one hand. That left the knife fairly close to his stomach. I could stab him, I realized. Throw my body into his as hard as I could. If I did, that knife would slice right through him.

Well, more through his side than anything, but the theory was the same. I took a breath, then hesitated.

Did I really want to do that?

An instant passed, and then it was too late. Using his free hand, he wrenched at my fingers. The knife fell to the floor, and he kicked it under the desk. Still holding both wrists in one hand, he wrapped the other arm around me, turning us both as he pushed my body toward the door.

At first, I thought he meant to march me down the hallway, presumably to gloat about how he'd beaten me. He caught the door instead, closing it with a crash. Then he shoved me against it, catching my hands with his again, pinning my wrists up and over my head. His big frame pushed into mine, trapping me, making it very clear that a five-foot-four-inch woman was a hell of a lot shorter than a man taller than six feet.

Eli had *seriously* worked out in prison.

I'd noticed how much he bulked up. Not that I liked noticing it, but I'd definitely noticed it. Now I felt it. Felt it in ways that reminded me that this wasn't the first time he'd pinned me down.

Hadn't been able to get the last time out of my mind, either, no matter how hard I tried to erase that particular memory.

"You need to settle the fuck down," he said, his eyes dark and hard, his gaze boring into mine. But his hips pushed against me when he said it, and I felt the length of something against my stomach.

At least part of him wasn't pissed off.

"Or what? You already won, asshole," I said, glaring up at him. My chest pushed against his as I tried to catch my breath. God. This sucked, because I wanted him. Wanted him in ways that just weren't right, because nobody should fantasize about fucking their mortal enemy. All I could think about was him sliding into me, though.

Deep inside, I clenched, feeling empty.

Then I caught his scent.

Shampoo. Not a man's shampoo, either. That was a woman's shampoo, which meant he'd spent the night with someone and then used her shower this morning, I realized.

God, what an asshole... The poor girl probably had no clue that he would never bother to call her. Odds were that he already had someone else lined up for tonight, and now here he was, grinding on me. Would I leave my scent on him, or would the next in line think that shampoo told the whole story?

It was a good reminder. Eli didn't even pretend to be decent. He never had.

"I *hate* you," I said, putting every bit of my rage and bitterness into my voice. His hips angled closer, and his cock pushed into me.

The place between my legs tightened, and my breasts felt full. A trickle of sensation wound its way along my spine. God must hate me because Eli had always made me feel this way. I'd fantasize about him at night, then hate him during the day. Because no matter how much I fantasized, he never paid attention.

I could hate him or fight with him all I wanted, but the problem was, any time we touched, he made me weak. Suddenly, I didn't want to kill him anymore.

I wanted to slide my arms around his neck...and then jump up, wrapping my legs around his waist. I'd grind against him until his dick hurt. Need burned inside of me. I recognized it and hated myself for it because nobody but Eli seemed to work me up like this.

It wasn't that I hadn't had sex. I'd slept with several guys through the years. But no matter who I fucked, they never quite got to me the way Eli did.

And they sure as hell couldn't satisfy me.

Although he'd satisfied me that night... The thought was enough to light a fire inside, and I blinked, trying to ignore it. Eli gave a low laugh. His hips rolled against my belly, and that hard length got bigger.

"You know you want it," he said, the words soft and knowing. Need wrenched its way through me. He was right. I totally wanted it.

But I'd die before giving him the satisfaction of admitting it.

"You had your chance," I whispered. His hips rolled again. God. He was too tall. His dick was centered on my stomach, and because of that, he wasn't touching me where I needed to be touched.

Evil, I reminded myself. A flash of Lemur's tiny stuffed animal face filled my vision, and I felt new resolve. It didn't matter how sexy Eli was, or how many dreams I'd had about his cock slamming home into me.

This was the same person who'd kidnapped Lemur.

Then he'd *murdered* him, caring so little that he hadn't even bothered to notice where he'd thrown the innocent little creature's body.

I'd sworn a vow that day, one that I'd nearly broken five years ago.

I wouldn't be breaking that promise today.

Eli transferred my wrists to one hand again then dropped his free palm down to my face, cupping one cheek as his thumb brushed gently across my lips. Back and forth, the scrape of callused skin across softness called to me. My nipples hurt, and I found my hips rocking forward involuntarily.

Hungry…seeking.

"You want it," he said again, his eyes catching and holding mine. "I do, too. I jerked off a thousand times in prison, picturing you under me. I'd lie awake at night, hand squeezing my cock hard enough to hurt, wondering what it'd feel like to sink into your pussy. This thing between us, Peaches, it's real. It's been real for a long time. We need to make peace."

His voice was so soothing…

My eyes fluttered shut as his thumb probed my lips. I hesitated, then opened my mouth, sucking his digit inside. Then I rubbed the bottom of it with my tongue, pretending I was sucking on something else.

Eli groaned, then shifted, lowering himself before sort of scooping up and into me with his hips. The new position had to be uncomfortable as hell, but it left his cock right where it was supposed to be.

"Some nights, I'd think about that time you stole my car," he continued, his voice near hypnotic. "I remember the look on your face when I finally caught up to you. Jesus. You were so proud of yourself. I couldn't decide whether to strangle you or fuck you over the hood."

His thumb pushed in farther. I didn't protest, I just sucked it in deeper.

"You used to piss me off so much."

My teeth nipped his thumb, and he groaned. I'd heard that sound before…the night he'd gotten arrested. That's the noise he'd made when I unzipped his pants then slid my hand inside to discover how ready he was for me.

The skin covering his dick had been tight.

Painfully so. Tight and hard and ready to thrust deep inside of me, just like his fingers had been inside of me as we kissed.

You could let him do that right now… His thumb pulled back, then thrust into my mouth again. Deeper this time. One of my legs shifted to the side, my knee sliding up and along his thigh. Eli shuddered against me, hips bucking into mine.

I tugged at my arms, and he let them go.

"I'm going to kiss you," he murmured, pulling his thumb free. Then I felt his breath on my lips.

Opening my eyes just a little, I reached up, tangling my fingers in his hair. Then his mouth came down over mine. I latched on to his bottom lip with my teeth and bit Eli King as hard as I could.

For Lemur.

He gave a strangled shout and jerked back his head. That was a bad move on his part, because I was still firmly attached. One of my hands gripped his hair as the other slid down between us.

Just like I had that night.

But this time, I didn't reach for his cock.

Nope. This time, it was all about the balls. Catching them wasn't easy—the denim of his jeans protected them—but I managed to get enough of a grip that he stilled as I tightened my fingers.

"Jesus," he tried to say, but the word was all garbled. My teeth still held him, and the faint taste of blood filled my mouth. I took a moment to secure my grasp on his nuts, giving them a squeeze for good measure. Then I let his lip go, tugging back on his hair, studying his face.

Eli might be bigger, heavier, and better at fighting than me, but I was meaner.

"Do not think for one minute that I'm stupid enough to fall for your shit," I said.

"I could kill you," he answered, frustration and anger warring for control on his face. *Nice.* "Don't you get it, Peaches? You may think you're all tough, but you're just a little thing. You can't beat me like this."

"You sure about that?" I asked, twisting my fingers. It had to be killing him, but he didn't blink.

"Yeah," he said. "I'm sure."

In an instant, he'd somehow shoved his arm between us, then twisted around. I flew toward the floor and would've hit it, except he caught me, literally hoisting me over his shoulder like a firefighter.

"Let me go, you fucking bastard!" I shrieked, trying to figure out how I'd gone from literally having him by the balls to…*this*. I started hitting his back and kicking, then tried to lift my entire body up.

That got me a smack on the ass, which I did *not* find amusing.

Eli took three steps, then flopped me down onto the couch. A second later, he was on top of me, thrusting his knee between mine. My arms were splayed out above my head, held down firmly by his hands. His hips pinned mine. I saw a little trickle of blood coming from his lip. My tongue darted out, and I tasted copper on mine.

We settled into glaring at each other, trying to catch our breaths. Then he spoke.

"You are a fucking bitch, Peaches Taylor."

"You better believe it," I replied, narrowing my eyes. "You think you've won—"

"I *have* won."

"But I'll find a way to make your life a living hell," I continued, ignoring his declaration. Eli snorted.

"You've been making my life hell since I was seven years old. That has to change if you want to keep working here."

"What makes you think I'd work for you?" I snapped.

"You love it," he snapped back. "And you're good at it," he added, clearly reluctant to admit the truth.

But he was right. I really *was* good at running the bar. Way better than Gus had ever been. We had a whole new class of customers. Dancing on the weekends… I'd changed the entire model, and it showed.

"Damned right, I'm good at it. That's why I should be buying the bar right now. Not you."

"So we both know that you're good at managing the place," he continued, ignoring my other statement. "And we both know that I've been gone a long time. Gus can help me during the transition, but if I really want this place to succeed, I need you here. I want you to manage the place. Officially. You're already doing all the work. Might as well have the title and authority."

My jaw dropped. "Do you seriously think that you can just sweet-talk me—?"

"Shut the fuck up, Peaches!" he snapped. It startled both of us. I was the one who blew up. Not him.

"Just shut the fuck up," he repeated. "For once. Listen to me, okay?"

"So you can feed me some line of bullshit about *needing* me?" I asked, suddenly tired. "You don't need me, Eli. You've never needed me. All you need is your fucking club."

"What's that supposed to mean?"

I closed my eyes, wishing I'd been smart enough to walk out when Gus told me the news. That was my big flaw, I realized. I didn't know when to let go. Never had… "It doesn't matter."

"The fuck it doesn't," he said, giving my hands a jerk. His hips ground into mine, and I felt my legs spreading for him, even as I hated him. "Tell me what you meant."

Fuck it.

"None of you let me talk to the cops after they arrested you," I said. "I was *there*, Eli. With you. I don't know who really killed that guy, but it wasn't you. You had an alibi. *You were with me.* Hell, you were almost *in* me."

His cock hardened as I said the words, and without thinking, I circled my pelvis into his. We were both thinking about that night now, and it hurt. "After all those years of fighting, that night we were *together*. And then you let them take you away. I could've saved you from that, but you wouldn't let me. Why?"

My jeans were soft, and I felt every seam and bump inside his as he slowly rocked against me. He didn't say anything for long seconds, and I felt the waves of need building in me even as my frustration grew.

"I couldn't," he finally replied. "I just couldn't, okay?"

"Why not?" I asked, knowing I was giving myself away, and not caring. I'd spent the last five years wondering why a man would *choose* prison… A man with an alibi. Someone who'd been all but fucking me while the crime was committed.

The silence grew painful as we stared at each other, my eyes pleading with his for answers.

"I can't tell you," he whispered.

That's what he'd said then, too.

"Let me go."

"No."

"Let. Me. Go," I said again, my voice harder. "I see how it is… I give up. You hear that? I. Give. Up. You win, Eli. You get the bar. You get to keep your secrets. But you don't get to fuck me, and you don't get to serve me bullshit and expect me to thank you with a smile. Let me up. I'm leaving."

He didn't move, and we lay there for a moment—him hard between my legs. Me, pinned beneath him. We were near each other like always, I realized. But we'd never really *be* together. Then he spoke, and his words shocked me.

"I don't want you to leave."

"Let me up," I whispered again, refusing to listen. To wonder why he'd say something like that. It didn't matter. Whatever game he was playing, *it didn't matter.*

Eli suddenly rolled to the side, then reached down to offer me his hand. I ignored it, sitting up, trying to think. He shook his head, then sat down next to me.

"I'll give you two weeks' notice," I said after another long pause. "You don't deserve it, but I've put way too much work into this bar to just walk off and let everything fall apart. Gus hasn't been running things for the past few years. I have."

"I know," Eli replied, his voice serious. "Gus knows, too."

Hearing the words hurt. More than I expected.

"Am I supposed to be thankful that he noticed?"

"Look, I know you're angry at him—"

"No, I'm angry at you."

"But he loves you. He's always loved you."

"Like he loved my mom?" I asked, turning to look at Eli directly. His eyes softened. We sat there for a moment, just staring at each other, and then the ridiculousness of the situation hit me.

"This is crazy," I said, glancing around and taking in the office. I'd shredded the poster. The chairs had been knocked over, and I'd smashed the keyboard into the wall.

Eli snorted.

"Your mom would've set the place on fire."

"My mom *did* set the place on fire," I replied, feeling a little smirk stealing across my mouth. "I feel like I failed her. I didn't even make it out of the hallway."

"The customers do a pretty good job of tearing up the bar itself," Eli said casually. "You're more of a specialist. Although I appreciate the fact that you didn't kill the computer. I don't know how good the backup system is."

I glanced over at it, thinking of all the hours I'd put in working on it. "It's set to automatically back up to the cloud. I do the books. Did you know that? Gus hasn't worked on them in years. You're fucked, Eli."

My smirk turned to a full-on smile at the thought.

"I know," Eli admitted, and he smiled, too. "Jesus, you're never boring. Don't leave, Peaches. Manage the bar. I'll pay you more. We can make this work."

"How much more?" I asked, allowing myself to consider it. Could I work for him? I wasn't sure...

"I don't know," he admitted. "I haven't seen the books. I don't even know how much you're getting paid now. You'll have to tell me."

I thought about it, glancing up at what remained of the poster. It'd taken months to find, but less than a minute to destroy it. Not that I regretted it. Gus deserved it. He really had fucked me over...just like he'd fucked over my mom. But I still needed a job, and Eli would be offering me a very nice salary, I decided. A very nice one, indeed.

Otherwise, he could figure out the passwords on his own, because Gus sure as hell didn't know them. Idiots. Both of them were idiots.

"I'll give it a month," I told him thoughtfully. "But don't fuck with me, Eli. I'm serious. Or next time, I really will slit your throat."

"I believe you," he replied, and it almost sounded like he did. I'd have to retrieve that survival knife before he remembered it. Hide it somewhere good. "I'm just glad you didn't have one of those knives when we were kids."

I considered the thought of my five-year-old self with a ten-inch steel blade, then nodded slowly.

"Yeah, you're probably right about that. I had more of a temper back then."

Eli coughed, then looked away. I could tell he wanted to say something. I waited, but he kept his mouth shut.

Wow.

Maybe he'd gotten a little smarter in prison. I still hated the bastard, but I could take his money. For a while, at least. Hard to know with an old building, though. So many things could go wrong. Maybe there'd be a fire, after all.

We'd just have to wait and see.

Chapter Four

Thirteen years ago

~Eli~

"So, I heard there's a party at the clubhouse this weekend," said Holly. She smiled up at me, twirling a strand of hair around her finger. My eyes slid down, noting just how perfectly her tits filled out the front of her spaghetti strap tank top.

Technically, those weren't allowed—too much of a distraction. I could appreciate a good distraction as much as the next guy, but seeing Peaches wearing one earlier today had been enough to convince me that maybe the school should enforce that rule.

Being a helpful kind of guy, I'd pointed that out to Peaches. Fortunately, her arms were a lot shorter than mine. Made it easy to just hold her back when she tried to punch me.

"You're too young for a club party," I told Holly, which was kind of unfair. We were the same age. But I wasn't like other high school seniors. I'd been born old, and the club was in my blood. The guys would eat Holly alive.

She took a step closer, the move almost predatory. Then a wave of her perfume hit me. Heavy and musky, and not in the good kind of way. I flashed back to the last time I'd fucked her.

That shit was potent, and it didn't wash off.

"You sure about that?" she asked, raising a hand and placing it on my chest. Then her eyelashes started flapping. The move was supposed to be sexy, but it came off more like a butterfly having a seizure.

"Not gonna happen," I said, reaching up and gently pushing away her hand. Then I turned toward my locker. We still had a few minutes to make it to class, but the conversation was over.

Holly didn't take the cue to leave.

"What do you think Mark sees in her?" she asked, sounding annoyed.

"Who?" I asked, then realized I'd fucked up. I knew damned well who she was talking about. Peaches and Mark McDougal had been dating for a month. Quarterback and cheerleader—the perfect cliché. They made out in the hall and sat together at lunch. It was cute and adorable and complete bullshit.

Mark was fucking at least two other girls on the side.

"Peaches Taylor," Holly said. "I know she's hot as hell, but she's not gonna fuck him. She's still a virgin."

"Why do you care?" I asked, keeping my tone casual. I'd been wondering if Mark had gotten to her yet. Fucker. "Nothing to do with us."

Holly laughed. "This school is too small for you to get away with that, Eli. You're hung up on her."

I turned back to her, frowning.

"My uncle was kinda her stepdad for a while. He likes me to keep an eye out for her. That's all."

Holly raised a brow, calling silent bullshit. "You're not going to invite me to that party no matter what I say, right?"

"Nope."

She rolled her eyes.

"Okay, then will you at least mention me to Bryce? I heard he's single again."

"You don't want to hook up with Bryce."

"Not your decision to make," she countered. It was a good point, but Bryce was thirty years old. Not only that, he had four kids by four different women. Holly and I had never been anything more than casual, but I had enough respect for her to think she could do better. "And I know it's none of my business, but if you turn around right now, you'll see what Mark's about to do to the girl you don't care about."

Keeping it casual, I grabbed my bag and then turned around, taking in the hallway full of students doing everything but studying. Part of me noted Jenny Woelfel and her pack of mean girls huddled off to the right, sharpening their knives.

On the left was a clump of cheerleaders and football players. Peaches and Mark were with them. Mark stepped into Peaches' space, herding her back toward the wall of lockers, using his bulk to surround her.

He might not've fucked her yet, but he would soon.

I swallowed, reminding myself that she was sixteen now. It wasn't my place to step in, regardless of what Gus said.

"Wanna tell me again that you're not hung up on her?" Holly asked, her tone light and mocking. I didn't bother denying it this time. Jesus Christ, but I hated the way Peaches looked at him. Of all the guys she could choose, why *him*?

Mark McDougal was a piece of shit.

A spoiled, entitled asshole who'd never had to work. Never suffered or been alone.

Never had to fight for a goddamned thing.

His dad was a lawyer. Sleazy as hell, and a bully, too. Fucker sued anyone and everyone, draining their pockets until they settled with him just to make it end. He'd even gone after one of my club brothers over a fifty-dollar oil change at his garage.

Now, Mark was leaning down into Peaches, one of his hands rubbing up and down her arm as he whispered something to her.

She flushed, all pretty and nervous and giggly. Clueless. She was nothing more than a trophy for him. A pretty, popular toy to fuck for a while until he got bored or left for college.

Sure, I wanted to fuck Peaches, too. But I also wanted good things for her. Well, mostly good things. I wanted to do a couple of bad things…

Mark's head tilted, and I watched as his lips covered hers. The kiss started off soft, but within seconds, their bodies were pressed together all the way. Then the hand that'd been tracing her arm reached down to find her ass, gripping one cheek tightly. If she'd been wearing anything but jeans, his fingers would be buried in her ass. Whatever hatred I'd felt before doubled. Tripled.

I didn't just hate the fucker, I realized. I wanted to *end* him.

Someone gave a wolf whistle, and Peaches froze. Then her hands pushed at Mark, almost frantic as she realized what a show they'd been putting on. For an instant, the asshole ignored her attempt to get away.

Please, God, give me this one. Let me kill him.

I'd just stepped toward them when Mark pulled away. Peaches' cheeks were still flushed and red, but this time, she looked embarrassed.

Christ, she must have it bad. She'd forgotten where they were, and if Mark had any doubt about how easy it'd be to take her before, he wouldn't now. Just then, the asshole glanced in my direction. Our eyes met, and he gave me a slow smile.

Fucker reached down and grabbed his sack, deliberately adjusting himself.

Holly hadn't been wrong. The school was too damned small. Mark knew I wanted Peaches. I'd warned more than one guy off of her this past year.

"What'd you do to piss him off—?" Holly said, but I didn't catch the rest. I was already striding toward Mark, hands fisted with angry tension. Someone needed to teach that pissant a lesson about respect.

That's when Peaches stepped in front of me, pushing a hand against my chest.

"Stop," she snapped, and the softness on her face was gone. This wasn't Peaches, the girl who'd just gotten embarrassed by kissing in the hallway.

Nope, this was my old enemy. The tough, strong girl who'd put snakes in my bed.

Instinct kicked in.

"What's the matter?" I asked, taunting her. "Afraid your boyfriend can't take me? Or is it that he isn't enough? I wasn't planning on fucking you with my mouth for an audience…but if you're wondering how it's done right, I could help you out."

Her eyes flashed, and the hand on my chest pulled back to slap me. I caught it, blocking her easily enough.

"Go to hell, Eli," she hissed. "This is my life. You don't get a vote."

"That's where you're wrong," I said, savoring the anger on her face. Mark stepped up behind her and put a possessive hand on her shoulder.

I was bigger than he was. Tougher, too. I knew it, and he knew it, but if we got into a fight here, I'd be the one hauled out by the cops.

"Careful," I said, catching and holding Mark's gaze. Peaches might stand between us, but she was short enough for us to stare each other down. "She's club property, you know?"

"Shut the fuck up, Eli!" Peaches said.

"This isn't one of your little games," Mark added, sounding bored. "I'm not scared of you, King. You bikers may think you run things around here, but you're just a bunch of tweakers and losers."

Peaches stilled, and I felt storm clouds gathering. Then she jerked her arm free of mine and turned on Mark.

"Gus is like my dad," she snarled. Good girl. Her mom and Gus might've broken up, but she still found her way out to our place at least one night a week. Peaches and Gus were family.

Mark had just fucked up. Big time.

"I didn't mean it like—" he tried to say, but she cut him off with a wave of her hand. I smiled as the bell rang. All around us, students seemed torn between heading to class and watching the show.

"Most bikers are really great people," she continued. "And Gus doesn't use drugs. Don't go saying shit about people unless you actually know what you're talking about."

With that, she shoved Mark out of her way. Every step she took radiated anger as she snagged a backpack leaning against one of the lockers. She slung it over her shoulder with one hand and raised the other to flip us off over her head as she joined the stream of kids heading to class.

Within seconds, the hall cleared out, leaving Mark and me still facing each other. We'd be late unless we got moving, but I had an advantage over him in this particular situation. He cared about his grades. Me? Not so much.

"You hurt that girl, and they'll never find your body," I said casually, offering him my best smile. "Consider yourself warned."

Mark swallowed, and I almost laughed. He might act tough, but the fucker was a coward once the witnesses were gone.

"She doesn't belong to you," he said, his voice wavering. My smile got bigger.

"Nope, but she belongs to Gus," I replied, casually cracking my knuckles. "Don't think of me as a guy you go to school with. Think of me as Gus's eyes and ears. And fists."

Mark's mouth opened, then closed again.

Like a goldfish.

I couldn't help myself, I started laughing. My work might be done for now, but I couldn't help but catch him with my shoulder hard enough to knock him off balance as I walked away.

Mark started cussing, scrambling to stay upright. I didn't bother turning around to see if he'd fallen. I was too busy enjoying the moment.

Football practice was ugly that afternoon.

I wasn't really the football type, but I was big and fast. Had been a starter on offense *and* defense since junior year, although given how small the school was, it sounded more impressive than it actually was.

Coach had been in a bad mood, and it was contagious. First, he'd bitched us out for lack of team unity, then he'd divided us into two teams to scrimmage. Things got dark when Mark's friends decided to put all their energy into tackling me instead of going for the ball.

Things got even darker when I sacked Mark's ass on the next play.

Coach really lost his shit then, and we spent the rest of the afternoon running the bleachers. Fucking brutal. By the time we hit the locker room, I was ready to kill someone. Grabbing my bag, I cut between rows of lockers toward the door.

That's when I heard Mark's voice on the other side.

"Think I'll fuck her in the ass while I'm at it," he said, and he sounded just as angry as I felt. I stilled, something deep inside of me going cold and dark. One of his friends laughed, but it sounded nervous.

"Dude, are you sure about this?" another guy asked. It sounded like Troy, but I wasn't sure. "She's into you. It's gonna be easy. Why take the risk?"

"It's not a risk," Mark answered. "She won't even remember it if I do it right. And if she does, it'll be her word against mine. Not like anyone will believe her. She might be pretty and popular, but she comes from trash."

She comes from trash.

Fuck.

Me.

Time seemed to slow because I could see the whole thing playing out in my head. Peaches might be into Mark, but she was still a virgin—not necessarily a sure thing. And now he had something to prove.

A detached section of my brain noted that I should talk to the club president after I finished with Mark. The asshole apparently had roofies, and he'd gotten them from someone—someone that didn't belong to us.

The club wasn't a big fan of freelancers setting up shop in Hallies Falls.

And I wasn't a big fan of Mark fucking Peaches in the ass, either.

He was still talking, but I tuned him out, considering my next step carefully. Didn't really matter what the details were at this point. I knew everything I needed to know about Mark and his plans.

The only open question now was one of control. Realistically, would I be able to control myself enough not to kill him?

It was a serious question.

If I jumped him in the parking lot, there'd be witnesses. That was bad because I might find myself arrested. Or suspended. That'd complicate my life considerably.

On the other hand, if there were witnesses, I'd *have* to control myself, and there'd only be so much time before the cops arrived, which put a natural limit on the damage I could inflict.

"Can a girl on roofies give a blowjob?" one of the guys asked, and I had my answer.

Better to get arrested for assault than murder. And if I ever caught Mark McDougal alone, I'd definitely kill him. I'd take him down in the parking lot. That'd send a message to every guy in the high school, too.

Peaches Taylor might not come from money, but she had people.

People who'd stand up for her.

She'd probably hate me for doing it, but that was nothing new. She'd always hated me. Wasn't like I had much to lose.

Wasn't like she'd believe me if I just tried to warn her off, either. Hell, if I told her the sky was blue, she'd insist it was green just to spite me.

Decision made, I started toward the door again, making for the parking lot. Mark still needed to shower, which meant I had some time to kill. Might as well use it productively. That fancy car his daddy'd given him was real shiny. Too shiny. A few scratches would do it some good…

Maybe I'd write a little message with my keys. That way, all the girls would know what to expect from him on a date. Hell, it was practically a public service.

Just the thought made me smile. Pulling out my cell phone, I hit the call button. Gus answered on the third ring.

"What's going on?" he asked, gruff as always.

"Probably gonna need some bail money," I told him. "And a lawyer."

Gus sighed, the same one he gave when he realized he needed to swap out a keg. "All right, then. I'll call the club. This about Peaches?"

"You don't wanna know the details," I replied, tilting my head to the side so I could crack my neck. "I'll take care of this one. No reason both of us should get locked up tonight."

Springdale Public Library
405 S. Pleasant
Springdale, AR 72764

Chapter Five

Present day
Two weeks after getting the news about the bar

~Peaches~

"So, I ran the numbers," I said, handing my mom a can of Diet Coke. Then I climbed up onto the couch and crossed my legs, leaning against the arm.

"What numbers?"

The question came from James. He walked casually across the living room, coming to a stop next to my mom. His hand settled on her shoulder. I scowled because he wasn't supposed to be part of this conversation. The fact that he'd married my mom didn't make him part of my family.

"I was just calculating how many pairs of used panties I have to sell online before I have enough money to buy the Starkwood," I said, my voice sweet.

James raised a brow.

"And?" he asked. I frowned.

"And, what?"

"How many would you have to sell?" he elaborated, his face solemn. Holy shit. Did he think I was serious? For the thousandth time, I wondered how my crazy, wild, fun-loving mom had gone from Gus to a guy like this.

An accountant.

Well, a former accountant. He'd gotten into land development and real estate years ago, but spreadsheets were his first love.

"About fifteen thousand," I told him. "But I hear you can order them in bulk for discounts."

"Please tell me you just made that number up," my mom said.

"Nope," I admitted, wishing she was right. "I researched it. You can get about twenty-five bucks a pair on a fetish site…and you can do upgrades. Like, if I don't wipe—"

"I'll give you twenty-five dollars not to finish that sentence," Mom said, shuddering. James absently rubbed her shoulder, his expression thoughtful.

He *always* looked thoughtful.

I wondered if the expression ever changed. Like, say someone was going down on him, would he still look so…thoughtful? I pictured it and then realized that my mom would be the one doing the going down. And now *I* was the one shuddering in horror.

"So, you'd need three hundred and seventy-five thousand dollars to buy the bar?" James asked. "Based on gross, of course. You'd probably have to sell closer to twenty thousand pairs, given shipping and overhead. I don't know what the Starkwood's cash flow is, but three seventy-five seems low to me. Does it include the building, too?"

I studied James for a moment, trying to decide if he slept in a bed, or if Mom just shut him into a pod at night to recharge. Mom took a drink, sighing. She knew what I was thinking. We'd had this discussion before. But no matter how many times she tried to tell me that James was the man for her, I couldn't see it.

It wasn't that he was ugly. The guy was okay to look at. But there was no life in him. He was more of a robot than anything else…

I realized the automaton was waiting for an answer.

"It includes the building, the land," I told him. "All of it. At least, that's what Gus said would work when we talked about it. I don't have the income to qualify for a loan, but Gus said he'd carry the contract. Eli can give him cash, though."

"Hmm…"

"It doesn't matter, baby," Mom chimed in. "You don't want to buy that place anyway. Trust me on that. There's a lot more to running the Starkwood than you think."

"I've been managing it unofficially for years," I pointed out. "Still am. Although I haven't gotten my raise yet. Not until the papers are signed. Eli promised me more money than Gus is willing to pay."

"That's not fair," James said.

"Wow, thank you for pointing that out," I snapped. God, he annoyed me. I understood that Mom had left Gus for a reason, but seriously…this guy? "But there's a part of me that's kind of glad it's not finalized yet. Something could happen. The sale could still fall through."

"It sounds like it's a done deal," Mom said. "Doesn't matter if the papers are signed. The decision has been made. I'm not surprised, either. Like I said, there's a lot going on there. The Reapers will want Eli in charge. Wouldn't matter how much you offered Gus."

I opened my mouth to argue with her, then closed it again. Could she be right?

Gus had given me the bad news right after he finished meeting with two club presidents. I hadn't really questioned that because I *never* questioned what the club was doing. That was how I'd been raised.

Suddenly, it seemed painfully obvious.

Gus wasn't the only one involved in this decision. The Reapers must have something to do with it, too. Mom widened her eyes at me as if she knew what I was thinking and gave me a don't-say-it look. I shot a quick glance at James. He'd pulled out his phone, apparently fascinated by whatever was on it.

Fucking robot.

"Mom, you think you can help me in the kitchen?" I asked pointedly. She nodded, gently nudging James to the side so she could stand up. He hardly seemed to register the movement.

We passed from the living room through the large, formal dining room that'd always seemed too big to me, and then moved into a kitchen so perfect it could've been in a magazine.

The house was beautiful, but it had no soul.

Just like its robot master…

I leaned back against one of the countertops, ready for some answers.

"Why are you so against me buying the bar?"

"I've never wanted you to buy the bar," she said, clearly confused. "I've told you that all along. Since you were ten years old."

"Yeah, but you never told me *why*. And tonight, it sounded like you knew something. Something about the Reapers."

Mom took a deep breath, clearly considering her answer carefully.

"Seeing as I shared a bed with Gus for many years, it's safe to say I know a great deal," she finally said. "I know you care about him. You trusted him, and you counted on him. But ultimately, Gus couldn't be the man *either* of us needed. He failed both of us. That's the reality you've never wanted to hear."

The words hit me with physical pain. My eyes started to burn, and I knew they had to be getting red. Mom sighed, and I could see her eyes getting red, too. Absently, she raised her hand, taking a drink from the can of pop she'd brought with her from the living room.

"Why did you marry James?" I asked softly. "Were you just looking for someone who'd be the opposite of Gus?"

Mom's eyes went wide, and she choked. Her shoulders started shaking.

"Mom?" I asked, concerned. She made another choking sound, holding up her hand as her lips pressed tightly closed. Now, her whole face was turning red. I needed to help her, but I had no clue what was wrong.

A drip of Coke escaped her lips, running down her chin. She wiped at it, still shaking.

That's when I figured it out. Mom wasn't choking. She was *laughing*. Laughing with her mouth full of pop, trying not to spray it across the room.

Not the reaction I'd expected.

Her eyes caught mine, dancing as she held her fingers to her lips. I felt my own giggle starting. Apparently, that made it worse because she made sort of a smothered squealing sound, then turned away, stumbling toward the sink.

My giggles turned into full-on laughter as she sprayed out her drink, gasping for breath. Then we were both laughing. I still wasn't quite sure what was so funny, but it didn't matter.

It'd been too long since we laughed together.

"I looked up the property parcel and ran some more numbers," James announced, wandering in from the dining room. *What the fuck?* For some reason, that seemed even funnier to me, and a fresh burst of laughter exploded.

Mom gasped for breath, wiping her mouth with the dish towel that'd been hanging next to the sink.

"Would those be the panty sales numbers?" Mom asked, which set me off again. James looked between us and gave a deep sigh.

"No, those would be property values on the Starkwood Saloon," he said. "It's very good. The price Gus offered you, that is."

"James, stop right there," Mom said, her voice sharp. Ouch. Clearly, we were done laughing. "It doesn't *matter* what the price is. Eli is buying the bar. Peaches can't afford it."

"Of course, the price matters," James replied, seeming almost confused. Mom and I froze, sharing a look. I waited for him to explain. He didn't.

"Why does it matter?" I finally asked.

"Because that's a very lowball offer," James said, giving his phone another glance. "It's worth nearly that much just in the land. If he'll sell it to you for that price, you need to buy it. No question."

"Are you fucking kidding me?" Mom burst out.

"No, I'm not 'fucking kidding' you, sweetheart," James said, and he sounded funny. Not the usual, boring robot voice… No, this was almost flirtatious.

My stomach turned.

That was weird. He didn't flirt. He didn't tease, and he didn't play games. James was a *robot*.

"Peaches, I'll back you," he continued. "In fact, I'll even give you some room to negotiate. You can go as high as four hundred thousand. We can hammer out the details later, but if they haven't signed papers, now is the time to move. You should call Gus right now."

"No," Mom said, her eyes darting between us. "James, we've talked about this. You know why I don't want her there."

"I know why you left," he said, his tone gentle and very *not*-robotic. "And I know that you don't want her at the Starkwood. But she's already there, and has been for years… If Eli takes over, he's making her the manager. She loves the place, and she's not going to leave anytime soon. So, the real question isn't whether Peaches is going to stay at the Starkwood, it's whether she'll be working for herself or for someone else."

I stared at him, trying to figure out what the hell had just happened. Clearly, James had paid a lot more attention to my life than I ever realized. Not only that, I knew he was smart. He had money, too. Money he'd made in real estate.

Hell, that's why most people thought Mom had married him.

"Thank you," I finally managed to say, still stunned. "But, why?"

James raised a brow. "Because it's a good deal, Peaches. That's how I've always worked. I watch, and I wait. That way, I'm ready when a really good opportunity crosses my path. That's how I got your mother, you know. Took me three years to convince her to go out with me, but when she finally said yes, I was ready."

"He was," Mom said, smiling at him. "That was the most romantic date I've ever been on. He thought of everything…"

James set his phone on the counter, then caught my mom's hand, pulling her toward him. She reached up to cup his cheek, even as he leaned down to give her a soft, sweet kiss. Then their mouths opened, and shit got real.

Jesus Christ.

Mom and James were making out like horny teenagers, right in the middle of the kitchen. The whole damned world had gone crazy, clearly. I looked away, uncomfortable. There was a wet, smacking sound, followed by a soft moan.

"Um, you need to stop now," I said, shifting my feet awkwardly. The smacking noises continued. Turning my head, I stole a peek at them. Holy shit, was James' hand reaching for Mom's butt?

"Stop!" I said, horrified. "I can't do this. I can't watch you guys make out in the kitchen. What the hell is wrong with you, Mom? I'm your *child.*"

She pulled away from James just slightly. "You're nearly thirty, baby. I know this may shock you, but I'm not dead. I still like to have sex, and this is my husband. It's allowed."

James wrapped an arm around her, tucking her into his side. She sighed happily, and I threw up a little in the back of my throat.

"You're disgusting."

"We're in love," James replied, the words sounding incredibly weird and wrong in his robot voice.

Mom laughed at the look on my face. "You know how you asked me earlier if I married James because he's not like Gus?"

"Mom!" I hissed, wondering what the hell she was thinking, saying that in front of him. She laughed again, and this time, the sound was deeper. Sensual.

"I married him because, deep down inside, he's the man I need him to be," she whispered, and I realized that James was right.

They were in love.

My wild-ass, crazy mom was in love with an accountant who'd told me once that he didn't like motorcycles. Because they were too dangerous.

"Go talk to Gus," James told me, giving Mom another squeeze. "Make the deal. We'll figure out the details tomorrow. It'll be fair."

"Um, yeah..." I said, backing slowly away from them. I couldn't process this right now. *That's okay. You don't need to understand what just happened to take advantage of it. Just leave the house before they start making out again.*

"Peaches?" Mom said, catching my attention. She'd wrapped both of her arms around James again, resting her head on his chest. "There's another reason I married him, you know. The thing is, he's really good in the sack. I've always had a high sex drive, you know."

I turned and ran out of the room.

Chapter Six

~Peaches~

"Kinda desperate, coming here on your night off," Eli said as I walked up to the bar. "Usually, girls just text me when they want a booty call." His lips quirked up in a smirk.

"Go to hell," I replied absently. Where was Gus? The place was mostly empty, just a few of the Reapers hanging out in one of the corner booths. Megan was wiping down tables, and Eli was the only one behind the bar. I frowned, boosting myself up onto one of the bar stools. "Oh, and can I have a rum and Coke?"

Eli leaned forward on his elbows. "Too late. I already did last call for the night."

"It's hardly past eleven," I said, surprised.

"Slow night." He shrugged. "Decided to close early."

"I've been trying to convince Gus that we should close earlier when it's like this for the last three years."

Eli's mouth quirked up, radiating smugness.

"Gus isn't in charge anymore."

My stomach dropped. "Does that mean you signed the papers today? I thought they weren't ready yet."

Eli raised an eyebrow, but he didn't give me a direct answer. Instead, he grabbed a couple of shot glasses and set them out between us. Then he grabbed a bottle of Crown Royal from the shelf behind the bar.

"Eli, did you sign the papers?" I asked again, feeling nervous. He filled the shot glasses. This was starting to look like a celebration, which didn't make sense.

They weren't supposed to finalize things until next week.

"Got them today," he said, and I heard the triumph in his voice. That fucking bastard... It wasn't enough for him to take the bar from me. Nope. Now, he wanted me to *celebrate* with him. This was about him winning. Again. "Already looked everything over. We'll sign them tomorrow morning at the title company. Grab your drink, Peaches. It's time for us to make a new start."

Eli caught my eye, raising his glass in a toast.

I briefly considered throwing the shot in his face because I'd be damned if I would concede defeat. If the papers hadn't been signed yet, I still had a chance to make my offer. Eli didn't need to know that, though. So, I gave him a strained smile and forced myself to give his glass a token tap. Together, we downed the shots.

He reached for the bottle and started pouring again.

"Are you trying to get me drunk?" I asked, wondering if he had a deeper game. "Because I stole bottles of this shit all the time in high school. It'll take more than two shots."

"Not true," he said. "You always went for the crappy vodka. Easier to water down. Cover the crime."

He had me. I'd totally done that.

"You liked it mixed with Dr. Pepper," he added, lifting his glass again and grinning at me over the top of it.

"How the hell do you remember that?" I asked, startled. Eli held my gaze, and for once, he wasn't challenging me. He looked almost...friendly. Not luring-me-into-a-false-sense-of-security-so-he-could-destroy-me friendly, either.

Friendly for real.

It freaked me out.

"I'm not trying to get you drunk," he said. "I'm just feeling good about things. It's been frustrating, waiting to take over. I'm ready to have it settled. I know you're not happy about how things turned out—"

"Understatement."

"I get it," he continued. "The situation wasn't fair. But we have a chance to start things over again. Do it right. Both of us love this place. You've been working here for seven years. And starting tomorrow, you'll be the manager. Do you really want to be at each other's throats for the next ten years? Don't you ever get tired of fighting?"

I didn't know what I'd expected him to say, but that wasn't it. I grabbed the shot, downing it quickly. The first one hadn't done much, but this one set my head spinning.

Or maybe that was just the sound of Eli being reasonable.

"Let me ask you this," I said carefully. "If I'd won, would you be willing to celebrate with me?"

Eli didn't pretend not to understand.

"Yes, I would," he said. "But this wasn't about winning."

I raised a brow.

"Peaches, do you really think I want to take your dream away from you?" he asked. "I didn't plan for you to get hurt, but Gus promised me this bar a long time before he ever talked to you about it. I have dreams, too."

"What you mostly have is money," I said, feeling my frustration and anger rise. "Money you didn't even earn, for the record. I've spent the last seven years busting ass, and we both know I've been managing it for a long time. And don't tell me this was your dream. Nobody *made* you go to prison, Eli. We both know you didn't kill that guy. I was your fucking *alibi*. And yet, for some reason, *you chose prison* over staying with us—"

Horrified, I snapped my mouth shut, wondering where the hell that'd come from. Eli studied me, one of the little muscles in his jaw tensing.

Then his gaze flicked toward something behind me before he caught my eyes again.

"Let's talk in the office."

Sliding off the stool, I turned and saw that Gus had just walked through the door. Gage was with him, along with more club members.

Eli rounded the bar, catching my arm.

"Office," he repeated, tugging at me. I took a moment to consider. I'd come to see Gus, not Eli. But this many club brothers all together, right when the bar was closing…that struck me as odd.

"Are the Reapers having a meeting tonight?"

"Doesn't matter," he said. "We need to finish this conversation. Privately."

Gus caught my eye and offered a casual wave before turning back to Gage. A couple of the prospects started sliding tables together.

"You're done for the night," Eli said, and I blinked, confused. I thought he wanted to talk some more.

"Don't you need someone to serve the bikers?" Megan said. I hadn't even noticed her walking up to us. I swayed a little, realizing that those shots were hitting me a little harder than they should have…

I hadn't eaten dinner. Come to think of it, I hadn't eaten lunch, either.

"I think Gus and I can handle drinks for the club," Eli told her.

"Peaches is here if we need help."

"What makes you think I'm willing to help?" I said, tugging at my arm. His fingers tightened, and he pulled me toward the office.

"You don't need to help," he said as we walked down the hall. "I was just getting rid of her. Now, let's finish that talk."

He opened the door, then pushed me toward the couch. Part of me wanted to argue with him, just out of habit. But I also wanted to hear what he had to say. So, I sat down, crossing my arms over my chest. Eli settled next to me, right in the middle of the sofa. Typical. He had a whole damned piece of furniture to sit on, but he had to take the spot right next to me. Making himself comfortable, he leaned back and turned toward me.

"You know what the club is," he said. "Right?"

"I know all about the club," I replied, wondering where he was going with this. "I grew up with the club. I lived in Gus's house before you, remember?"

"Jesus, why do you always have to bring that up?" he asked, clearly frustrated. "I was a little kid. I needed a place to live, and that room was big enough for both of us. Where was I supposed to sleep? The kitchen? Your bedroom was where they put me. I did what I was told."

"Did they tell you to kidnap Lemur?"

He blew out his breath in exasperation. "I was ten years old, Peaches. I'm sorry I took your stuffed animal. I've apologized about a thousand times now, but I don't have a fucking time machine. I can't fix it."

"You cut off his tail and kept it as a *trophy,*" I hissed.

Eli looked away. "That was shitty. Ten-year-olds do shitty things."

"You hung it on your rearview mirror in high school."

He shifted. Clearly, the guilt had gotten to him. I paused to savor the moment.

"Eighteen-year-olds do shitty things, too," he admitted. "And if I remember correctly, you stole that car. Smashed one of the fenders."

"It was a rescue operation," I pointed out. "I had to retrieve Lemur's remains and give him a dignified burial. The car was just collateral damage, something that never would've happened if you hadn't desecrated his corpse."

Eli closed his eyes for a moment, taking a deep breath. Then he opened them again.

"You know that the Reapers are more than just a bunch of guys who like to ride motorcycles together, right?"

"Everyone knows that."

"Yeah, but you grew up with it," he continued. "When we say we're brothers, those aren't just words… And part of that brotherhood is watching each other's backs. That's how this thing works."

"Were you watching someone's back when you went to prison for a crime you didn't commit?"

"Do you really expect me to answer that?" he asked. "Didn't we just cover this? You *know* how things are with the club. And you know we don't talk about this shit. What the hell do you want from me?"

"I want answers!" I said, my voice rising. "You call them your brothers. Brothers *love* each other, asshole. When you love someone, you don't let them throw away their lives in a prison cell!"

"That's not what happened."

"Then what *did* happen?" I demanded, shifting sideways on the couch, facing him. "Because I remember that night. We were drunk—which is the only reason I started kissing you, by the way—and you were nowhere near where that guy died. Why did you leave that night, Eli? And how the hell did you end up under arrest for something you couldn't possibly have done?"

He opened his mouth to answer, but I cut him off.

"Don't you *dare* feed me any more bullshit. I know *exactly* who and what the Reapers are—and what they're not. They didn't order you to take the fall for someone. You made that choice. You say you want us to be friends. That we should work together? Prove it. Give me an explanation."

The words hung between us, along with a thousand memories. Eli's eyes darkened, his expression intense as he caught my shoulders, pulling me toward him.

"Peaches, if there was any way to tell you, I would," he said, holding my gaze.

"You're a liar," I whispered. "You don't care about this bar, and you don't care about me."

"That's not true."

We stared at each other for long seconds, at an impasse. Then he shook his head slowly, muttering, "Fuck it."

Suddenly, his mouth was on mine, and I felt his hand sliding into my hair, gripping it tightly as his tongue thrust into my mouth. Sensations exploded through me—need and desire and just a hint of triumph. Because whatever it was that we'd felt for each other all those years ago, I hadn't imagined it.

We'd been frantic that night, ripping at each other's clothes, years of sexual tension driving us into a frenzy. This time, Eli's kiss was different. Not the crazed, sloppy mouth-fucking he'd given me at that party. This was deep and hungry.

As if he were starved for my taste.

The office door opened.

"It's time for the meet—oh, shit…"

I jerked away from Eli to find Gus standing in the doorway. He wore a strange expression. Not upset or angry, exactly. I'd have said he was pleased if he didn't look so uncomfortable.

"Give us a few?" Eli asked, his voice husky.

"Yeah," the old man said, glancing back down the hall. "You got ten minutes. People still need drinks, and I'll take my time pouring them. Join us after you put her in her car. She shouldn't be here tonight."

Gus shut the door, leaving Eli and me sitting next to each other. I felt stunned. Almost raw. I'd come here to make Gus an offer on the bar. Not to do…this.

"I don't suppose you want to pick up where we left off for another eight minutes or so?" Eli asked, trying to lighten the mood. I reached up and touched his face.

Remembering.

"You hurt me," I said after a long pause, forcing myself to drop my defenses. "You really hurt me, Eli. And setting whatever was between us aside, I could've *saved* your ass. You wouldn't let me, and you still won't tell me why. How can you not see how fucked-up that is?"

He swallowed.

"Yes, I did," he replied, and his voice was more serious than I'd ever heard it. "It was a shitty thing to do to you. Not to mention, stupid as hell. I'd give anything to go back to that night and change things. Wasn't like I planned it, Peaches. Nobody ever thought it would go that far."

His eyes were dark. Haunted, even. He was telling the truth.

"So, now what?" I asked.

"That's up to you," he said. "We can keep fighting. Try to run the bar together. Probably go crazy until you end up slitting my throat for real. Either that, or I'll lose my shit and fire you. Regardless, it'll get ugly."

"And what's the alternative?" I asked. "Let me guess. I walk away from the Starkwood?"

He gave a short, dark laugh.

"Yeah, like that's gonna happen."

Fair enough.

"We could try making peace," he said. "For real. Neither of us has to give up on our dreams if we work together. It doesn't matter whose name is on the deed, Peaches. We can be partners."

For an instant, something melted inside of me. If we were partners, then I wouldn't have to be on guard all the time. He drove me crazy, but it always left me feeling more alive.

What would it be like to truly work together?

Wait.

"It doesn't matter whose name is on the deed?" I asked, forcing myself to think things through.

"Not really," Eli said, catching my hand. Tingles danced across my skin where he touched me. I forced myself to ignore them.

"So why does it have to be *your* name?" I continued, keeping my tone casual. Eli raised a brow. "If it doesn't matter, I mean?"

"Um, because I have the money to buy it?" he said.

"How much?"

"How much, what?" he asked, and I caught the first hint of suspicion in his eyes.

"How much money did you get from your dad's settlement?" I asked, pulling away from him. "And how much is Gus charging you?"

Eli frowned. "Where are you going with this?"

"Let's just say, for the sake of argument, that I have enough money to buy the bar from Gus," I said slowly. "Do you think he'd sell it to me? If I could beat your price, I mean? Seeing as it doesn't really matter whose name is on the deed…"

Eli studied me.

"You've got money from somewhere, don't you?"

I took a deep breath, hoping I wasn't ruining everything. Eli was right. We couldn't go back and undo what'd happened in the past. But if we could make peace now… I thought about that kiss again, and how good it'd felt to be open with him.

"Yeah," I said slowly. "I've got money. I'm going to make Gus a cash offer. You say you want to be partners. Prove it. Tell me what you're paying him, and I'll tell you if I can beat it."

Chapter Seven

~Peaches~

Eli didn't answer. He looked away from me, then sighed and shook his head.

"I knew it," I told him. "You're so full of shit, Eli King."

"It's more complicated than that."

"No, it's not. Tell me what you're paying, and I'll see if I can beat it. Put up or shut up."

He wouldn't look at me. "You don't want to do this."

"You don't get to decide what I want," I said. "I'm twenty-nine years old, but you and Gus still treat me like I'm a child."

"That's not true."

"He just told you to *put me in my car*," I said, feeling my temper rise. I reached out and caught his chin, forcing him to look me in the eye. "I was sitting right here. Next to you. But when he wanted *me* to do something, he told you to do it. Like I'm your dog or something. It's getting a little bit old. Let me make my own fucking choices for once."

Eli blinked, clearly trying to figure out what the hell to say. Finally, he settled on, "You're not a dog."

"I *know* I'm not a dog. So, answer the fucking question."

"Three hundred and twenty-five thousand dollars," he said. "That's the settlement. It earned a little more sitting in the bank. I'm paying him three hundred and forty thousand for the land, the building, and the business."

"That's lower than he told me."

"Well, he was planning to carry the contract for you," Eli said. "This is cash."

"I can pay more than that," I told him. I studied his face, waiting for him to react. I expected anger—like I'd felt when I thought he'd won—or maybe frustration.

What I saw instead was worse. Much, much worse. Sadness, and maybe even a hint of…pity?

No. No fucking way.

"Peaches, he's not going to sell to you. It's about more than money."

The words were physically painful to hear. Another gut punch, almost as bad as when Gus had pulled the rug out from under me the first time.

"Why not?" I demanded.

"You know why."

"It can't be that special," I said, feeling almost anguished.

"What?" he asked, confused.

"Your *penis*. What the hell is it about having a penis that makes you more qualified to own this place than I am? Because as far as I can tell, that's the biggest difference between us."

Eli opened his mouth, then closed it again, seeming at a loss. Someone knocked on the door.

"Gus says it's time."

Eli blew out his breath in frustration, then ran his fingers through his hair. That made him look sexier, of course.

Almost like God was giving me the middle finger.

"Go," I snapped, pushing myself up and off the couch. "Go have your fucking meeting. Just don't think I'm taking your word for it. If Gus wants to turn down my money, he can do it in person. Oh, and I'll put myself in my car, so you don't need to worry about that."

"It's safer if I walk you out," Eli said.

To my horror, I felt tears welling in my eyes. Not only that, my nose felt runny. I grabbed the bottom of my shirt and pulled it up so I could wipe, flashing Eli in the process.

"Oh, fuck off," I said, hating myself for crying. Crying always made me feel weak. "You've seen my boobs before. I'm going to take a few minutes before I leave. Calm down. I don't want anyone to see me like this, okay? You owe me that much. I'll just sneak out the back when I'm ready."

"All right," he said, clearly reluctant to leave.

"Don't worry," I said. "I won't tell Gus you let me off the leash or make a mess in here. I'm a good dog that way."

"Peaches—"

"Shut the fuck up, Eli. Just shut the fuck up and leave me alone."

* * * *

~Eli~

I couldn't focus for shit on what Gage was trying to tell us.

I kept thinking about Peaches, and how much better she'd tasted than I remembered. Fucking hell… The night we'd almost had together, it'd been amazing. As the years passed, though, there were times when I doubted my memories. Kissing a girl couldn't feel that good. Not in real life.

Except it did with her.

Peaches and I had always had chemistry. It was probably what kept us at each other's throats. Although I could think of better uses for her throat. Christ, just the thought was enough to set me off. My jeans tightened, and I shifted uncomfortably in my seat.

Gus tried to catch my eye from across the table, but I ignored him, just like I'd ignored the seat he'd saved for me. I was still processing what Peaches had told me about the money. Well, trying to process it. Hard to think when all your blood kept pooling in your crotch.

I needed to get that girl into bed.

Soon.

Fighting with her was fun, but it wasn't enough. We needed to fuck. Repeatedly. And that couldn't happen until we resolved this whole situation.

Gus wouldn't sell the bar to her, no matter what she offered. I knew that for a fact, and it had fuck-all to do with her being a girl. He owed me in ways she couldn't begin to understand.

But even if he wanted to take the deal, the club would shoot him down. Her point about not having a dick was valid on that front… The Reapers might respect her—they'd never have settled on her as a compromise after I'd gotten locked up, otherwise—but she'd never be one of them. They'd take my side, even if Gus didn't.

"Eli?"

I looked up to find everyone staring at me. Shit. Gage must've asked a question, and I hadn't even noticed.

"Sorry," I told him. "Can you repeat that?"

"I was curious about the paperwork," he said. "Gus says you'll be signing things tomorrow. Anything I need to know?"

Well, shit. That was one hell of a loaded question. I glanced at Gus. I loved him, but he'd really cocked up this time.

"Yeah, I'd say there's a complication," I said. "Big one, actually."

"What's that?" Gage said, clearly surprised.

"Peaches Taylor is going to make Gus a cash offer tomorrow," I told them. "She says she can outbid me."

Silence fell across the table.

"There's no way," Gus said after a long pause. "She doesn't have any money. She doesn't have any credit, either."

"I suppose she could be lying," I replied, shrugging. "But I can't think of any reason she would. And since she doesn't have her own money, that means there's another party in the mix. Gotta be her stepdad."

Suddenly, everyone got really quiet.

James Carrington wasn't Gus's favorite person. Not that he'd have been okay with anyone who married Peaches' mom, but Carrington also happened to own the property next to Gus's house. There'd been a disagreement over an easement about ten years back.

I sat back, waiting for Gus's reaction. Surprisingly, he didn't blow up.

"Doesn't matter," he said. "We already made a deal."

"Don't you think Carrington will find it strange, considering he's offering more money?"

"We'll say it's part of your inheritance," Gus countered. "You're my only heir. It's a family deal."

"I think we should run it by the club lawyers," Gage said thoughtfully. "Carrington has a lot of connections, and the guy's like a fucking bloodhound when it comes to money. Tinker sits on the hospital board with him. She says he drives everyone crazy. Because if something looks even a little bit off to him, he'll spend hours tracking it down. We don't want that kind of attention."

"I've kept the books clean," Gus protested. "There's nothing for them to find. We should just sign the papers first thing in the morning. Then it'll be too late for her to make an offer. Problem solved."

Jesus. He was doing it again.

"You should talk to her," I said bluntly. "We wouldn't be in this mess if you'd communicated with her in the first place. I know you don't like it when she gets upset, but this is ridiculous. Grow a pair and own your shit."

Dead silence fell across the room. Conflict was nothing new among brothers, but Gus was essentially my dad. I'd never publicly questioned him before.

"Not your decision, Eli," Gus finally said. I'd expected anger, but the words came out sounding almost weak. "And there's no shit to own. I'm under no obligation to hear her out."

"I'm under no obligation to sign the fucking papers tomorrow morning."

"Is this really club business?" Gage asked, looking between us. "Or is it personal? Because it sounds personal."

"It's personal," Gus said. "Eli and I can talk after the meeting."

"It's not personal," I countered, starting to feel angry. "The club has a stake in the Starkwood. When you decided to sell to me, you got club approval first. I'm assuming that means you talked to them about carrying a contract for Peaches, too."

"He did," Gage confirmed.

"She does the bookkeeping," I told Gage. "At least, she does the books we show the IRS. When you agreed to sell to her—something nobody bothered talking to me about until after the fact, by the way—you were planning to bring her into the loop, right?"

"Moot point," Gus said. I ignored him.

"So, you were willing to trust her as a business associate," I continued. "She's been a friend of the club her entire life. If her stepdad is going to cause trouble, wouldn't it make more sense to meet with her? Maybe give her an explanation? I know you're afraid of pissing her off, Gus, but she loves you. She wouldn't set you up. Carrington won't get suspicious if he thinks she's the one who changed her mind. So, change her mind. Problem solved."

"I'm not afraid of anything," Gus snapped.

"My bad," I said, raising my palms. "I can't imagine why I'd think you were... What time did you want to sign those papers again?"

Someone snorted with laughter, quickly turning it into a cough.

"Peaches doesn't need an explanation," Gus said, sounding more defensive with every word. "You made your point, Eli. I fucked up by not telling her that things had changed. That was a mistake. But beyond that, she's just an employee. It doesn't matter what she thinks."

"She thinks you treat her like a dog."

He gave me a confused look. "A dog?"

"A *dog*," I said. "And I can see why. You're treating her like a pet, not a person. She's worked here for seven years. You made a deal with her to take over, and then you jerked it out from under her, saying you needed cash. She got cash. Now, you're trying to hide instead of talking to her. It's like kindergarten."

"Eli..." Gage said, his tone warning me.

"All due respect, Gus, but have you considered that it's my ass on the line once the papers are signed? Peaches may love you, but she hates me. If you burn her again, I'll have to let her go. Is that really what you want?"

Gus looked stunned. "You'd fire her?"

"No," I said, hoping I wasn't making a huge mistake. But I couldn't forget the pain on her face. She'd said that I hurt her. And I had. But it'd been Gus hurting her, too.

He needed to be part of the solution.

"I won't be able to fire her," I told him. "Because I'm not buying the bar. Not unless you hear her out. You need to listen to her, and then you need to explain why you're selling to me in a way that satisfies her. Then I'll sign."

Gus's face flushed, and I heard a few mutters.

"He can't share club business," Gage said. "You know better than that, Eli."

"Then I guess Gus can't retire yet after all," I said, leaning back in my chair. "Gonna be a real bitch, running this place without me *or* Peaches. Good luck with that."

"I took you in when you had *nothing,*" Gus said, his voice rising.

"And I went to prison for a crime *you* committed." Everyone went silent. The words were true, but I'd never spoken them out loud before. I'd be lying if I said it wasn't a relief. But then I took a deep breath and focused on the only father I'd ever known. "I love you, Gus, and I appreciate everything you've done for me. But I already gave you five years. This time, you need to clean up your own mess."

Chapter Eight

Six years ago

~Peaches~

"You know," I said, speaking very slowly so the words wouldn't slur. "I think I like the *drinking* alcohol better than I like serving it."

McKayla nodded, her face serious.

"Way better," she replied, handing me her liquor bottle. "And that's not the only thing we've been doing wrong."

I took a deep swig. Tequila. Wasn't sure how much I'd had, but it was enough that it didn't burn going down anymore.

"Doing what wrong?" I asked.

"Working," she said, swaying to the side. I caught her arm so she wouldn't fall over. Not that it'd hurt her much. We were already sitting on the floor for reasons that'd made sense to me in the moment.

"We should stop *working* here," McKayla continued. "And start *drinking* here. You know, instead of working. I just think that'd be better. Can I have the bottle again?"

I frowned, considering the idea as I handed over the tequila. Challenging, with all the party noise. The buzzing in my head didn't help either. Every time I caught a thought, it tried to wiggle away.

"Drinking does seem way better than working," I agreed. "But we also need money to *buy* the drinks. So, if we stop working here, we'll probably have to work somewhere else. Otherwise, we'll run out of money."

"Oh," she said, her smile fading. She fell silent. I took the opportunity to survey the room—well, as much of it as I could see from the floor—pleased with how many people had shown up. All the Reapers, of course. Not just the locals, but quite a few from other chapters. Most of our friendly regulars, too.

The only one I hadn't seen yet was the birthday boy. Gus.

McKayla grabbed my arm, shaking it.

"What?" I asked.

"I've got the best idea! We don't need our own money to buy drinks. We just need someone to buy them. Anyone, really. So, why couldn't we just sleep with men to get alcohol? That's way more efficient than working."

"Tough call," I said slowly. "Because that sounds a little like prostitution."

"Nope. Prostitutes earn money. We wouldn't be earning money, just booze. And we'd keep it classy, too. No well drinks."

"Hard to argue with logic like that…"

"I know, right?" she said, giggling. McKayla was many things. Sweet and cute. Friendly.

Ultimately not much brighter than a chicken, though.

"So, assuming we decide to do this—and that's a big *if*—then who do you want to sleep with first?"

"Eli," she said with a little too much enthusiasm. "I'd really like to fuck Eli. But only once you're done with him. I follow the code."

I scrunched my nose at her. "I'm not interested in Eli. He smells like dirty feet."

"Yeah, I don't believe that," she said, reaching for the bottle again. "If you weren't interested, you wouldn't hang out with him so much."

"I hang out at Gus's house, which is where Eli happens to live," I corrected her. "Between that and work, I see him a lot. Doesn't mean I like it."

"Does that mean I can have him?" she asked, perking up.

I frowned. For some reason, I didn't care for that idea. *Don't think about it. Thinking is almost always a bad thing.*

"Okay, whatever," I said. "Just be sure to use like, six condoms. Because he's probably got all kinds of cooties."

McKayla gave a high-pitched squeal.

"You're amazing, Peaches. I love you!" she said gleefully, raising the bottle for a drink. But instead of swallowing, she lowered it, glee replaced by grief. "Oh, this is the worst. How could something so terrible happen in such a beautiful moment?"

"What?"

She tilted the bottle upside down between us. Nothing came out.

"The tequila disappeared."

"How did *that* happen?"

"Someone must've grabbed it while I was distracted. Then they drank all of if before putting it back in my hand, all without me ever noticing..."

I pictured Indiana Jones swapping out a bag of sand for treasure, and a snorting laugh escaped. McKayla shot me a dirty look. "Don't make fun of me. It could've happened."

"Yeah. Definitely the most likely explanation."

She sniffed. "Doesn't matter what happened to the booze. We need to focus on what's actually important—finding another bottle. Fast. Otherwise, we're at risk of sobering up. That's not okay."

"Once again, very hard to argue with your logic."

"Exactly," she said, nodding slowly. "Let's go get more tequila."

Standing up turned out to be a lot harder than I'd expected. My left leg had fallen asleep, and I'd been sitting on something sticky. Not only that, but by the time I completed the process, I couldn't quite remember why I'd needed to get up in the first place.

Fortunately, the music was good, and people were starting to dance. Not only that, I loved dancing. Always had. And now there was a dance floor right in front of me when I needed it most.

Clearly, God wanted me to go shake my ass for a while.

Who was I to argue with *God?*

An hour later, Gus still hadn't arrived.

The party was fantastic—even without the birthday boy—and I was having a blast. I'd danced with all kinds of people. Well, mostly women, but some of the younger guys, too. It seemed like half the state knew Gus, and they'd all shown up to party with him.

This included at least forty members of the Reapers Motorcycle Club, plus their old ladies. They'd come roaring into town earlier that day in groups, meeting up at the state park campground before forming a convoy to the Starkwood. Others had joined in behind them, and now there had to be at least a hundred motorcycles parked outside.

My ears were still ringing from the noise they'd made when they pulled into the lot. Or maybe they were ringing from the music. It was slowing down now, and people had started coupling up on the dance floor.

Seemed like a sign to me—time to rehydrate. Only water, though. I'd worked up a sweat. Winding my way through the crowd, I made for the bar.

That's when I spotted Eli.

He sat on one of the stools, surveying the party as if we existed for his entertainment. To his right sat Tinker, and just past her was her man, Gage. I'd always liked both of them. My appreciation for McKayla was fading, though. She'd squeezed herself into the space between the stools to Eli's left, resting her hand on his chest possessively.

Did it bother me? Absolutely not...although I couldn't see them together for more than a night.

Eli needed someone smarter than McKayla.

Someone who could keep him in line.

None of my business, really, but I still needed water, and the best spot for flagging down the bartender was probably that gap between Eli and Gage's old lady.

"Do you mind?" I asked Tinker, choosing not to acknowledge Eli's presence.

"Not at all," she said with a big smile, scooting over. "It's a great party, Peaches. You did a good job planning it."

Eli shifted, and his elbow caught me. Returning Tinker's smile with one of my own, I elbowed him back.

"Thanks," I said. "Although I didn't actually do very much. Gus planned most of it himself. Said what he really wanted was to see the rest of us having fun. Although I did pick up the cake earlier today."

Eli jostled me again, and I nearly fell into Tinker. Asshole.

"I'm getting some water," I told her. "Do you want anything?"

"I'm good," she said, raising her beer. Using my shoulder, I shoved Eli as I leaned into the bar, waving down the bartender, Ethan. I didn't know him very well yet—he was new to the Starkwood—but he'd been doing an okay job so far.

"Hey! Can I get some water?"

He nodded, and I turned around again, catching Eli with my shoulder another time. He looked at me, then leaned in toward my ear.

"You trying to cock-block me?" he asked, jerking his head toward McKayla.

"Oh, I didn't even notice you sitting there, Eli," I said brightly. "And McKayla's with you! Hi, McKayla!"

I gave her a little finger wave, and she finger-waved back, giggling. Then she stopped waving, and her hand dropped down to his stomach.

My eyes followed, noting how the faded jeans couldn't quite hide his package. Easy to see, with his legs spread wide like that. Then her hand slipped lower, sliding down his hip to rest against his inner thigh.

Ewww.

"Got your water, Peaches!" Ethan said, his voice pitched loud enough to carry over the chaotic noise of the party. I turned back to him, thankful for the distraction.

The water tasted good. Almost unnaturally so. Guess I hadn't realized how thirsty I'd gotten. Enough to chug the whole thing in one gulp.

I set the glass down to discover that Eli had swiveled the stool to face me. McKayla had disappeared. *Must be smarter than I gave her credit for...*

"Don't blame me just because she ditched you," I said. "She probably heard that you're a murderer. Nobody likes a murderer."

That's when I noticed Ethan standing in front of us. I think he'd been reaching for my empty water glass, but now he seemed frozen. Horrified, even. Well, fuck. If he couldn't roll with a joke like that, he'd never make it at the Starkwood.

"She's talking about a stuffed animal," Eli told him. "It was when we were kids. She's obsessed with it. I've told her to seek professional help, but she's too proud. Sad, really."

Ethan nodded, although the move was hesitant. Fair enough. Eli was a big guy with a tough reputation. Throw in the fact that he was a Reaper, and I could see why Ethan might be nervous.

"Eli's right," I said, catching Ethan's eye. "I was teasing him about something that happened when we were kids. He's just a big softie inside. Like a marshmallow, only less flammable."

I nudged him with my shoulder playfully. He bumped me back—just a little harder—and then I slammed my shoulder into him, all the while holding Ethan's gaze and smiling.

"So, where the hell is Gus?" Eli asked. "I thought he was supposed to be here by now."

"Hell if I know," I said, shrugging. "He'll get here when he gets here. Think I'm gonna dance some more. If you're very lucky, I'll let you dance with me."

"No dancing. McKayla's out there, and I'm afraid she'll jump me or something. I'd rather avoid that, all things considered."

"I thought you were into her," I said, thinking about her hand on his thigh. That might've been her idea, but he hadn't seemed unhappy about the situation. "You said I was cock-blocking."

"That was before I smelled her breath," he said, winking at me. "Or maybe I just wanted to piss you off. Either way, she's not my type."

"And what would your type be?" I asked, curious. He'd always fucked around, but as far as I knew, he'd never had a serious girlfriend.

"I like 'em with a little more spirit," he said, catching and holding my eye. "McKayla'd be fun for about ten minutes. Then I'd get bored."

"Really?" I asked, raising a brow. "Because I heard that you only need five. Seven, max."

He laughed, and I caught Ethan eyeing us again. I leaned into Eli.

"I'm not so sure about the new bartender," I said, pitching my tone low. "Seems like he spooks easily. Might not be tough enough for a place like this…"

"He wants to fuck you. And he doesn't like me because he knows he doesn't have a chance while I'm around."

Now I laughed. "Yeah, right. Like I'd ever fuck you."

"You'd fuck me before you fucked him," he said, his voice dry. I had to agree. Ethan was skinny. Stringy, almost. Bad skin, and hair that never looked particularly clean.

"You won't think I'm hitting on you if I agree, will you?"

"Nope. I can always tell when you're hitting me because it hurts, and then I wake up with bruises the next day. Let's go shoot darts."

Catching my hand, Eli pushed off the stool and pulled me through the crowd toward the back hallway. Gus's office was on the right. The storeroom was to the left.

I'd always seen it as a magical wonderland of pretty bottles and kegs to climb on, complete with a fort we'd built out of liquor boxes. The finishing touch had been a dart board that we'd stolen from the main bar. Most of the time, we'd been pretty good about throwing the darts at the target instead of at each other.

Well, maybe not *most* of the time, but at least half…

Astoundingly, neither of us had ever gotten hurt during those epic battles for storeroom supremacy. Okay, so I'd stabbed him in the butt once. But it'd been an accident. Mostly.

Eli pulled a set of keys out of his pocket and unlocked the door. I reached for the light switch. He caught my hand.

"No, let's play in the dark. Like when we were kids."

"I'd sort of forgotten about that," I whispered, stepping into the room. We'd always kept the lights off. It made it harder for the adults to track us.

Now, I was one of those adults, and the storeroom had long since lost its magic. The bottles weren't treasures, and our fort had been broken down and recycled. But I knew for a fact that the dart board and darts were still here. So was the old wingback chair where I'd sat and read so many books. As my eyes adjusted, I saw the faint light shining through the two high-set windows on the far side of the room.

I couldn't remember the last time we'd actually played here. It'd been a long time. The darts and the board were still here, though.

Eli reached to the top of the shelf and grabbed an old shoe box. He opened it and pulled out a dart, handing it to me.

"What are we playing for?" I asked, stepping up to the silver duct tape that marked our line on the floor. Raising my hand, I sighted carefully on the bullseye. This was going to be a tough game, I realized. There was just enough light to see the target clearly, but not quite enough to see it well...

Oh. And I was still fairly drunk.

That probably wasn't going to help.

Eli hadn't answered the question, so I decided to ignore him and focus on my game instead. I took a deep breath, pulled back my hand just the slightest, and—

"How about a kiss?" he asked, his voice loud in my ear. The dart flew off to the left, bouncing off the concrete wall next to the target with a clang.

Sabotaging motherfucker.

"That one shouldn't count," I protested.

"Of course, it counts," Eli said. He used one of his big arms to sweep me to the side. Now, it was his turn to step up to the line.

"You know the rules," he said, radiating smugness.

"The only rule is that we don't tell on each other," I said, trying to glare at him. Hard to glare when all you wanted to do was laugh, though. "Everything else is fair game."

"There's your answer," he replied, shooting me a grin. He raised his hand to throw. On a wild impulse, I jumped at him, wrapping my arms around his neck and smashing my mouth into his.

Eli swayed, dropping the dart as he wrapped his arms around me. I ducked down, sliding out from under him, laughing. I staggered backward, nearly tripping over the chair in the process.

"What the fuck, Peaches?"

This struck me as incredibly funny, which made me laugh even harder. So hard that I couldn't breathe, let alone speak.

"I wish... I wish you could see the look...on your face," I finally managed to gasp out, although it took a few tries. "And my dart is closer to the target than yours is. That means I'm first."

"Never gonna happen," he said, and while the words were angry, his tone was teasing. Eli was having a good time, I realized. Both of us were.

"That doesn't count as a throw. Nice try, but your timing was off."

I raised a finger, wagging it at him while making little tch-tch-tch noises. "The dart was in your hand. You raised your hand to throw, and then you released the dart into the air. That's a throw."

"No," he said. "You attacked me. Without provocation, I might add—" I snorted. "I dropped the dart as a direct result of that attack. That's a foul. Doesn't count."

"Only if you're following some set of rules," I pointed out. "I'd like to remind you that our only rule is that we don't tell on each other. Here's the good news, I wasn't planning to tell everyone about your shitty throw. But it definitely counts."

He narrowed his eyes. "Okay. You can go first."

I grabbed another dart, then stepped back to the line. Obviously, Eli was planning retaliation. I tried to watch him, but he moved behind me.

The back of my neck prickled like I was being stalked by a tiger.

"Don't worry," he said as I tried to aim.

"About you? Never."

Except I was worried. Because I could feel him back there. Lurking. Waiting to pounce. *Just focus on the target. He's playing mind games with you.*

Taking a deep breath, I tried to concentrate. The bass from the party was a dim thump in the distance. Occasionally, a laugh or a shout could be heard.

The only thing I couldn't hear was Eli. Those big feet of his were like skis. No way could he move without making some noise, right? Except Eli was very sneaky…

Spinning around, I found him leaning against one of the shelves, a good six feet away. This time, he wagged his finger at me.

"Paranoia is a sign of a guilty conscience," he said, offering a shit-eating grin. I took a minute to consider throwing the dart at him. It'd be satisfying, no question. But he was trying to get a rise out of me. I didn't want to reward that kind of behavior.

I turned toward the board again, raised my hand, and then screamed as Eli's arms came around me from behind. One landed near my waist while the other crossed my chest, immobilizing my arms in the process.

"Bastard!" I shrieked, trying to sound outraged. But he'd lifted me, and now we were spinning around. I couldn't remember the last time someone had spun me around like that. I'd forgotten how much fun it was.

It felt like an hour but was probably only a minute or so before he stumbled. We lurched backward and almost crashed into the shelf. Somehow, he managed to fall back into the chair. I landed on top of him, laughing so hard that my ribs hurt.

Or maybe that was just from his arms squeezing me.

Eli's grip loosened, his hands dropping to rest loosely on my waist. I relaxed into his bulk, strangely comfortable.

"Your hair is smothering me," he said, catching my wrists and putting them together so he could hold them in one hand. Then he reached up and caught my hair, trying to finger-comb it to the side.

"Sorry," I told him, attempting to lean forward. He let go for an instant. Then his hands were under my armpits as he lifted me like a rag doll, draping me across his lap. His left arm wound around my back. My legs draped over the arm of the old chair as his right hand reached up and slid into my hair.

He pulled my mouth to his, and a world of sensation exploded through me.

I'd thought about kissing Eli in the past. The man was sexy as hell— you'd have to be blind not to notice. Blind, deaf, and without a sense of smell, more accurately. Every time I'd imagined those kisses, they'd been terrifying because Eli was intense. He never did anything halfway, and I suspected his kisses would overwhelm me.

Instead, his lips somehow managed to be soft while still demanding enough to leave no question as to who was in charge in the moment. His tongue slid into my mouth before I even fully realized what was happening. I was too busy squirming, aching, almost desperate from the sudden surge of need.

Feeling his tongue plunge deep, all I could think about was that I needed more of him inside of me. For once, I didn't feel like I had to fight or question what was happening. I just opened to him, drawing him in, wrapping my arms around his neck and pulling him closer.

His head slanted, kissing harder now. I felt something hard under my butt and knew it had to be him. I shimmied my hips, savoring the way it made him shudder. He pulled away for an instant, and our eyes met.

"Jesus, but that feels good," he said in a strained voice.

"Let's not drag Jesus into this, okay?" I whispered, then lifted my head, trying to catch his lips again. I didn't even notice that he'd dropped his hand to my waist until he tugged my shirt free from my jeans. I expected him to go for my breasts. Instead, he found the back of my pants, sliding his hand under the waistband and plunging deep to grab the cheek of my ass with big fingers.

He stilled, studying my face.

"You have no idea how many times I've thought about doing this," he said. He lowered his mouth for another kiss, brushing his lips across mine. It was lovely, but I needed more. He was kissing me like we were making love.

I wanted him to fuck my mouth.

Catching his bottom lip with my teeth, I bit down. Not hard enough to break the skin, but close. He groaned, and his hand clenched on my ass. Then he grabbed my hair with his free hand, twisting it around his fingers before jerking my head to him, holding me still.

My entire body clenched, liquid and hot and ready to take him.

If he can do this with one little kiss, what else can he do?

I clenched at the thought, spirals of desire zipping along my spine. I had to find a way to straddle him. Rub against him. Fuck him. I ached for it, squirming against the cock prodding my ass, needing more, and needing it *now*. He groaned, and I couldn't tell if it was pain or pleasure. It didn't matter. All that mattered was getting him inside of me.

"Don't move," he muttered, pulling back on my hair for emphasis.

That should've pissed me off, yet somehow it just turned me on even more. Swiveling my hips, I tried to grind down on him. His hips bucked up almost instantly, and he moaned.

At least I wasn't the only one who'd gone into heat out of nowhere.

Nobody could be expected to sit still when they ached like this.

Still holding his mouth with mine, I rolled to my right, directly into his body. My legs swung down, one on either side of his strong thigh. I slid my hips back, experimenting with the new position.

Oh, that was… Really good. *Holy-fucking-shit* good.

We kissed like that for long seconds, me grinding against his thigh, him holding me by the hair with one hand. The other squeezed my ass, pulling my hips forward into him with every stroke.

It wasn't enough. I wanted all of him between my legs.

Eli must've been feeling the same way because he let go of my hair and pulled his hand out of my jeans. Before I could figure out what he meant to do, he'd wrapped his hands around my thighs from the outside. Then he stood up, lifting me as if I weighed nothing.

I shrieked, wrapping my arms tightly around his neck.

Hitching me upward, he pulled me into his body, sending my legs splaying to either side. I hissed as his cock found just the right place between my legs. Then he sat back on the chair, bringing me with him, and it all made sense.

Now, I straddled him, my legs spread wide, one hanging off each side of the chair, draped over the arms. He caught my hair again. I expected him to give me another of those devastating kisses. Instead, he pulled back, tilting my head to give him better access to my neck.

His other hand slid back down into my jeans. His fingers were still spread wide, but this time, his thumb landed deep, pressing between my cheeks.

I froze, uncertain.

"Nothing happens unless you want it to happen," he said, kissing my neck gently. He tightened the hand on my ass, pulling my hips into his, slowly guiding me back and forth along the length of his shaft.

Hunger pulsed through me…hunger and the realization that he was serious. Nothing would happen unless I wanted it to.

What we were doing right then was damned good. Near perfect. Wonderful and exactly what I wanted. But it wasn't enough. Grabbing the sides of the chair for leverage, I swiveled my hips into his, feeling the bulge of his cock in a whole new way.

Bet it would feel even better without all these clothes in the way.

"You say nothing happens unless I want it to happen." I tugged against the hair he still held. He let it go instantly. I lowered my mouth, giving him another kiss. "Pretty sure I want you to fuck me right here in the Starkwood Saloon storeroom."

His eyes darkened. I realized his lips looked unusually good. *Probably from me biting them…oops.*

"You're drunk," he said, lifting his hips to give me a better angle.

"I'm not that drunk anymore," I replied, even if it wasn't entirely true. I was definitely drunk. And thank God for it. Because there was no other way I'd have relaxed enough to kiss Eli King, let alone have sex with him.

And I really, really wanted to have sex with him.

"You sure?" he asked. He wanted it as badly as I did. I could tell. There was something so surreal and sweet about the thought of Eli caring enough to double-check.

Grinding down, I shuddered, wishing like hell I'd worn a skirt. Then I could just lift up enough for him to undo his fly, and…

"Yeah, I'm sure," I said, my voice husky.

Both hands caught my ass again, giving me just a hint of warning before he stood up. My legs wrapped tightly around his waist without bothering to ask for permission. I'd always known he was strong, but I hadn't even begun to imagine all the fun a person could have with that kind of strength.

He could fuck me up against a wall, then carry me into the bedroom over his shoulder, toss me on the bed, then fuck me again.

I'd never been so turned on in my life.

"Where?" he asked, looking around the room. "We could go to the office."

"People would see us," I said, laughing. "You can fuck me right here, on the floor. I don't care."

"It's dirty."

"You are such a girl," I said, still giggling. "You afraid your knees might get dirty? It may not be the most romantic of spots, but it's not like we're dating. And I know you've fucked quite a few women in here over the years, so don't even try to pretend you haven't. Either you lay me down on that floor and fuck me, or I'm going out to that party and finding someone who will. Your choice."

Eli's eyes flashed, and I knew it was all over.

"Let me down," I told him. He lowered me, sliding me down every inch of his body until my feet found the floor. Instead of stopping, I lowered gracefully into a kneeling position, catching the end of his shirt and lifting it just enough to kiss his stomach.

His entire body shuddered.

My hands found the fly of his jeans. I cupped my fingers around his erection through the fabric, squeezing it tight. Then I looked up at him, offering a teasing smile.

"No fucking way," he said, shaking his head slowly. "I can't believe I'm saying this, but don't even consider giving me head. You wrap that mouth around me, and I'll last all of five minutes."

"Yeah, I thought ten minutes was a bit optimistic," I said, blowing him a kiss. Then I reached down and caught my shirt, pulling it up and over my head.

The look on his face when he saw my bra was more than enough to justify what I'd paid for it. But when I reached for my pants, that's when things got good. He stilled, standing over me almost mesmerized as I slowly popped the button on my fly, then lowered the zipper. The fabric sagged, clinging to my hips. I gave a little shimmy, which was enough to drop them a couple of inches lower…

"Shit," Eli muttered, ripping open his own jeans. He grabbed his cock, fisting it as I very slowly, very deliberately slid my fingers down the midline of my body.

When I reached my panties, I dipped them under, finding my clit with my middle digit. I gave it a quick rub, my breath catching, and then pushed my hand down farther, my finger sliding through my cleft.

"Nice and wet," I told him.

Eli shoved down his jeans, then dropped to his knees in front of me. First, he kissed me, cupping the back of my neck with one hand while the other wrapped tightly around my waist. He started lowering me to the floor, then paused.

"Hold on," he said. Leaning back on his heels, he caught the bottom edge of his shirt, pulling it up and over his head. Shaking it out flat, he spread it on the floor next to us. "Better. Now lay down."

I took a second to kiss him one more time, then lowered myself to the shirt. Something felt really bizarre, and I realized that this was the first time I'd ever done anything Eli had asked me to do without fighting with him first.

His hands found my jeans, and I lifted my hips so he could pull them off, along with my underwear. Then they were gone, and he was crawling up and over my body until our eyes met.

"You sure you know what you're doing?" he asked.

"Most guys don't ask this many questions when a girl tells them to fuck her."

"Yeah, well those guys probably weren't raised in a house where they had to worry about finding snakes in their beds."

The words sounded angry, but the tone was teasing. Resting his weight on his left arm, Eli reached down between us with his right, finding my clit right away. I gasped, and my hips rocked toward him.

The tip of his cock brushed against me.

"You have no idea how long I've been waiting for this," Eli whispered. My hips curled toward him, and—

The storeroom door flew open, banging into the wall.

"Eli! Where the fuck are you? We got a situation."

"Don't you dare answer," I told him, somehow whispering and shouting at the same time. I twisted my hips up and into him a second time, and his dick slid into me about half an inch. *Goddamnit.*

"Eli, there's big fucking trouble. It's Gus."

That sounded like Gage. Shit. Normally, he'd just send a prospect if he had a message. There must be something seriously wrong happening with Gus. My stomach gave an anxious little flip.

"What's wrong with Gus?" I asked, nudging at Eli to let me up. He rolled off me, and I started feeling around for my clothes. Suddenly, the lights came on, blinding me.

"Turn off the fucking light!" Eli shouted.

"Eli? Is that you?"

"Yes, it's Eli. And Peaches," I said, trying not to let my tone waver. I pulled on my pants, trying not to think about how many people would figure out that we'd… Eli made a growling noise, and a muscle in his jaw started twitching. "We'll be out in a minute."

"Move fast," Gage said. "It's serious, Eli. I need your ass at Gus's house in the next ten minutes. Pipes is waiting in the parking lot. Leave your bike here. I got a feeling we'll need you on Gus's before this is over."

"Fuck!" Eli said, slamming the flat of his palm against the floor.

Someone was feeling grumpy about his blue balls.

"Breaking your hand isn't going to help Gus."

"No, but it might protect him," he said. "Because unless this little emergency of his involves him dying, I'll be tempted to finish the job. Then I'll have to deal with the body. That'll be a real bitch if one of my hands is broken."

"What a…heartwarming thought."

"Yeah, I'm all heart."

"I'm coming with you," I said. "If he's dying, I want to say goodbye."

"Gus is way too mean to die," Eli told me. "Lots of people have come after him through the years. Note that they're gone, and he isn't."

"I'm serious. I'm coming with you."

Eli stopped and turned toward me. His hands moved to my shoulders, giving them a gentle squeeze as his eyes caught mine. "This situation is club business, Peaches. I can't bring you with me just because you're my girlfriend. That's not how my world works."

I ignored his use of the word *girlfriend* and the hope that it gave me. "Sometimes I think your world is bullshit."

"Yeah, sometimes I think my world is bullshit, too," he said. "But it's the only one I got, so I'm gonna make the most of it."

Chapter Nine

~Peaches~

"I went to prison for a crime you committed," Eli said, his voice ringing through the Starkwood. "I love you, Gus, and I appreciate everything you've done for me. But I already gave you five years. This time, you need to clean up your own mess."

Holy.

Fucking.

Shit.

For an instant, I thought I'd heard Eli wrong. What he'd just said couldn't be true. No way. Except Gus had been late to his own birthday party. I'd seen him come through the back door with Pipes, right about the time Eli was getting arrested for murder.

Eli couldn't have gotten to the house until after the killing, I reminded myself. And the murder had definitely taken place. Somebody had offed the guy. So why hadn't I suspected Gus before now?

Probably because you didn't want to.

Eli's announcement was essentially a live grenade, tossed into the middle of the meeting. Now, everyone was arguing. I couldn't hear much in the way of details, but at least a few of them sounded pissed because they'd been left out of the loop.

Good to know. Probably meant that the Reapers MC hadn't been behind this particular shitshow.

I didn't hear Gus say anything in his defense, and I had no way of seeing his reaction. Couldn't see much of anything because the only place to hide was behind the long wooden bar itself. If I'd planned to spy on them ahead of time, I might've been able to come up with something more comfortable. Maybe built myself the roadhouse equivalent of a duck blind. But it'd never occurred to me to spy on a meeting before.

Ever.

I'd learned from a young age that when the Reapers were talking, it was time to disappear. Let the men do their thing and stay out of the way. That hadn't been a winning strategy for me.

Hadn't worked out so great for Eli, either.

If I'd gotten in the way a little more, maybe Eli wouldn't have gone to prison. I couldn't blame Gus for all of—

Wait.

Where the fuck did *that* crazy thought come from?

Of course, it wasn't my fault. The real villain here was clearly Gus, with a possible assist from the Reapers. My heart hurt to think about it. I wanted to find an excuse for him, but Eli had been sentenced to *twenty years* in the state penitentiary.

How could Gus even look him in the eye?

Eli was innocent. I knew that for a fact, and apparently, so had Gus. And, yeah… It was great that the Reapers had hired a fancy lawyer to appeal the conviction, but Gus still owed Eli five years of his life.

Damned right, he should have to clean up his own mess.

At least now I understood why Gus was selling low to Eli. Hell, he should be *giving* him the Starkwood.

The tone of the meeting had changed from argument to shouting match, but I didn't care anymore. I'd heard everything I needed to know. Now, it was time to get my ass out of there, before someone noticed me. I didn't think I needed to be afraid of the Reapers, but I'd never dreamt that Gus would let Eli go to prison for him either.

Mom had been right—Gus wasn't the man that either of us needed him to be. The thought twisted my heart in terrible ways, but I couldn't deny the reality.

No. You can't think about this right now. You need to focus on getting out and getting safe. Figure out your emotions later.

Right. Grief couldn't hurt me if I refused to feel it.

Thankful for the noise, I slipped out from behind the bar and headed down the hallway, moving quickly. Past the office, past the storage room. Through the back door and out into the parking lot. I made it the whole way in complete silence. Then my car beeped when I unlocked it, shattering the stillness outside.

Stupid noise almost gave me a heart attack. There was usually at least one prospect stationed out front during meetings like this, to keep watch over the motorcycles. I kept expecting him to come running around the building, possibly with guns blazing.

Nobody seemed to notice, though. Lucky for me, in addition to the regular parking lot, Gus had worked some sort of deal with the national forest, and we'd gotten permission to use one of their gravel lots for employee parking.

It made for a long walk in, but tonight, I was thankful for the distance. They'd have to be watching exactly the right spot to see me pulling out. I kept my headlights off until I made it around the big bend in the highway, though. Just in case.

I didn't plan on driving to Gus's house.

Okay, so I'd planned to go there originally, but only so I could make him a cash offer. Given what I'd just heard at the bar, that seemed fairly pointless.

Not to mention wrong.

Eli had literally done time for Gus. I'd probably have to shank the old man myself if he backed out. Not that I thought Eli was a great guy or something, but he was better than some. Most, really.

If you love him so much, why don't you marry him?

Good God. Now my own subconscious was making fun of me. If I had to put up with a voice in my head telling me what to do, at the very least, it should be male, with a sexy Irish accent... Maybe Jonathan Rhys Meyers, although I'd settle for Colin Farrell if I had to.

Thankfully, the gravel country road leading to Gus's house was right ahead. Less than five minutes later, I'd parked my car and made my way around the back of the old farmhouse, to the kitchen door, finding it open.

This wasn't a surprise because it'd never been locked the entire time I'd known Gus. Same with the barn, and the shop—something that had come up during Eli's appeal. Gus had claimed that not only did he leave his place open, but that he didn't have the keys to lock it even if he wanted to.

Anyone could've taken his pickup that night.

That's what he'd told me, at least. And I'd believed him.

Stepping into the narrow galley kitchen brought back a thousand memories. Me and Mom, baking cookies. Me and Gus, microwaving marshmallow Peeps. There were even memories of Eli and me. Most of them involved chasing each other with knives.

"How the hell did we never get seriously injured?" I said, feeling almost wistful.

This was crazy. As an adult, I could see that my idealized fantasy had never existed. Yet for some reason, I was still sad about losing it.

And I'd lost another huge chunk of it today, in Gus.

Opening the fridge, I found a can of Dr. Pepper, which made me smile. Gus was an idiot who'd cheated on my mom and sent Eli to prison in his place. Yet for some reason, he always had Dr. Pepper waiting in the fridge.

How could he remember to buy me pop, yet conveniently forget all about my mom whenever he'd fucked someone else?

Eli wouldn't do that. Or would he? No, he wouldn't. He was better than that.

Taking a large plastic tumbler out of the cupboard, I filled it with ice from the little plastic trays Gus still used because he didn't trust ice makers. He had one at the bar, of course. Said that's how he knew they couldn't be trusted, which had always amused me.

I refilled the ice trays with fresh water, then grabbed my pop and the cup before passing into the dining room. At least, that's what my mom had always called it. In reality, there was just one big room across the front of the house, divided into two sections—one for eating, one for watching TV. For years, any time I came to visit, Eli would have to sleep out in the "living room."

Walking over to the sideboard, I opened one of the doors and pulled out a bottle of vodka. I was old enough now that I didn't have to worry about how full it was. I still enjoyed the occasional drink, but I wasn't much of a partier anymore.

Not after Eli had gotten arrested.

A part of me had always wondered if he'd refused to let me talk to the cops because I'd been drinking that night. They might not have trusted a drunk girl with club connections.

I'd spent years wondering *what if*. Whenever I'd asked Eli about it, he'd always changed the subject.

Now, I knew the truth. None of it had anything to do with me.

Popping the tab on the Dr. Pepper, I filled the tumbler about halfway full, then topped it off generously with the vodka. Then I turned to face the room, raising the glass high for a toast.

"To the snakes!"

"What the fuck is it about snakes that turns you on so much?" asked Eli, who seemed to appear out of nowhere. "If it's a fetish thing, I'd prefer that you keep it out of the bar."

"Holy shit!" I yelled, so startled that I dropped the cup, sending pop and vodka splashing across the scratched wooden floor.

"Funny how you can carry entire trays of drinks over your head, but that one plastic cup is just too hard for you to handle when you're here."

"It's warped from the dishwasher. Kind of like you," I snapped, then realized what a rude thing that was to say. Apparently, I'd told myself that he was the enemy for so long that I'd programmed my body to keep up the hate, even when I wasn't feeling it.

"Sorry," I said. "Let's try this again. You said something about this cup, and how hard it is for me to handle. I just realized you're playing that game with me, aren't you?"

"What game?" Eli asked, pretending that he didn't know exactly what I was talking about.

"The one where we trick each other into saying things that can be used against us."

"Yeah, I think I remember that one," he said, offering me a lazy smile. "But I'm not playing it tonight. If something sounds bad to you, that's because you have a dirty mind."

"So, you're telling me that you can't see how me saying I can always handle hard—" I stopped talking, wondering if there was anything in the kitchen suitable to bash in his skull when I swung it around by its handle.

He burst out laughing. I flipped him off, trying not to smile. Or worse, start laughing with him, because…the thought seemed to hang there, right in front of me, waiting for me to own it. I swallowed. This was going to change everything.

Eli isn't my enemy. Eli is one of my best friends. I've always been able to trust him with my secrets, even when keeping them gets him in trouble.

And he's always been able to trust me.

"Tell me about the night you got arrested," I said, letting the game go.

He gave me a wary look. "You already know everything you need to know."

"Bullshit," I insisted. "Tell me the real story."

"No," he said, and his voice softened. "Peaches, it would hurt you, and there's nothing good that can come from it. It's time to let it go."

"Why?" I said, stepping over the river of Dr. Pepper and vodka. "You afraid it'll be too hard for me to handle? I can't believe I fell for that. Probably because it doesn't even sound dirty anymore. I can't decide if the culture has changed that much, or if we were just exceptionally sheltered children."

I took another step toward him, and then another, closing the distance.

"You were sheltered," he said, catching and holding my gaze. "Me, not so much. Gus took me in because my mom was into meth. I don't remember the worst of it. Your mom always said that was my brain protecting my heart. Because some things shouldn't be remembered."

"I'm sorry," I said, reaching my hand out to him. He took it, his big fingers wrapping around my smaller ones, strong and warm.

Eli snorted, breaking the moment. "You were sorry that you had to share your bedroom."

"I was *five*. Every five-year-old on Earth has anger management issues they're working through. By definition."

"And have you finally worked through yours?" he asked, the question playful but very real at the same time.

"Not all of them," I admitted, walking toward the big, comfy couch in the living room. I'd started sleeping down here once they'd taken Eli away. For some reason, stealing his bed hadn't felt right. "I still need to hear about what happened that night. When you got arrested."

"Why?" he asked. "Talking about it won't change anything."

I let his hand go, settling back into the center of the brown sectional. It didn't match the rest of the house on about a thousand different levels, but it was comfy, and I loved sleeping on it.

Eli sat next to me, stretching out on the long section that extended into the center of the room. It was more of a bed than a couch.

"One last chance, Eli," I said. He reached over, catching my hand. Something wild gleamed in his eyes as he tugged me toward him. I started to scoot in his direction when I realized that he was using sex as a diversion.

"No fucking way," I said, pulling my hand back. I wanted to glare at him, but it took just about everything I had not to crawl into his lap. "I want to hear it from you. All of it."

His gaze sharpened. "What time did you leave the bar tonight?"

I considered pretending that I didn't know what he was talking about. That's what I'd done when I *borrowed* his car my junior year. He hadn't fallen for it then. No point in playing games. Not now.

"The last thing I heard was you telling Gus to clean up his own mess."

Eli leaned back against the cushions, propping up his feet as he studied the ceiling.

"Then you heard the part that matters," he said. "What else do you want to know?"

"Everything. But I understand that some things aren't supposed to be talked about. I can respect that."

He rolled his head to look at me, raising a brow.

"Okay, so I can sort of respect it a little bit..." I amended. "And I know Gus needs to tell the story for himself."

"Very true," he said.

"You know, I worshiped him when I was a little girl. I knew he wasn't my real dad, but it felt like he was. Then you came along, and he didn't have time for me anymore. Somehow, I convinced myself that there was only room for one child in this house. I had to get rid of you."

"You may have mentioned that a few times when we were kids," he pointed out, his voice dry. "I think the most memorable time was that day at the pond. You threw popcorn out into the water and told me that was the only food I was allowed to eat."

"I was horrible," I admitted. "I know I was horrible. I shouldn't have treated you that way, but I was only five."

"C'mere," he said and held his hand out to me. I took it, letting him pull me over for real this time. He rolled up on his side, creating enough space for me to lie on my back, bringing us face-to-face.

It felt horribly intimate. I wasn't just looking at him. I was smelling him and feeling the heat of his body.

My hands lay folded across my stomach. He tangled his fingers with mine, softly rubbing his thumb across the tiny strip of bare skin that'd been exposed when my shirt rode up.

"Better," he said. "So, let's get this out of the way. I know you were a kid. I was a kid. Neither of us had any control, and both of us were scared that Gus would love the other one more. The big difference was that you had your mom on your side, no matter what. I didn't have anyone but Gus. That's why he chose me, Peaches. And if he hadn't done that, I'd probably be dead by now."

"Yeah, I realize that now," I told him. "But I couldn't see it back then."

"In fairness, I couldn't see it either. I was used to living one meal to the next, hoping we'd land in a safe place for the night."

I tried to imagine that, but I couldn't. Mom wasn't perfect, but she'd always been totally on top of the whole food/shelter/clothing thing.

Even when I started kindergart—

A sudden realization hit me, and I swallowed. Eli had lowered his head, bringing our faces closer.

"Eli, I have another question," I said slowly. "Why did you get held back in the first grade?"

"Because I'd never been to school before. Didn't even know the alphabet."

"Did…?" I paused, licking my lips. That caught his attention, which was probably a good thing given what I needed to ask him. "Did I make fun of you because you couldn't read?"

He pulled his hand free of mine, then slowly moved it up my center. It came to rest right below my collarbone.

"You made fun of me every single fucking day for two years," he said, the words slow and even.

If I could've rolled into a ball and ceased to exist, that would've been the moment.

"I don't think sorry quite cuts it," I said after a long pause. "I really was the worst."

Eli nodded his head, moving just a little bit closer. If I raised my head even an inch, I'd be kissing him.

"How come you don't hate me?"

"Well, I'm older than you," he said, sounding way too damn smug. "More mature. I like to think of you as this silly little butterfly that dances all sum—"

I crushed my mouth to his because after what he'd just said about me making fun of him, telling him to shut the fuck up was probably a bad move.

But listening to that butterfly shit wasn't a real option, either.

Fortunately, Eli didn't seem overly invested in continuing the conversation. Instead, he shifted his body and slanted his mouth down across mine, taking control.

There was a new power in him, I realized. One that had nothing to do with all that muscle he'd built while he was serving time. This strength was all mental, and I had a feeling it'd grown out of his need to survive.

My higher mind appreciated that and admired him for it. But in my gut, what I noticed first was how much that strength attracted me. I'd spent years thinking about what it might feel like, should I ever find myself under him again. Not that I'd have admitted that to anyone, including myself…but anytime he was in a room, I found myself fighting with him.

Fucked up? Yes.

Especially since memories were fickle creatures. Nobody felt as good as Eli had felt that night we'd almost had sex. My intellect understood this. My subconscious? Not so much. At one point, I'd read a book about retraining the brain, and decided to try writing letters to myself, explaining all the reasons that Fantasy Eli had nothing to do with Reality Eli.

Now, I found myself under him again, with my hands roaming his body as my legs begged to wrap around him. Time to face a hard truth—this was way, *way* better than I remembered.

The chemistry between us had always crackled. It was there when we kissed, taking charge in the same way it did when we fought. There was no denying it, either. Every time his lips brushed mine, desire scorched through me. Like wildfire.

But power and chemistry weren't the only things for me to appreciate.

Eli had always been a large guy with a big frame, and he'd had more than enough muscle the night they'd taken him away. Still, he'd gotten bigger while locked up. Not ginormous and bloated.

Just very solid.

It took a special kind of guy to pull off muscles like that without intimidating a girl, I realized. Eli could hold me down and do whatever the hell he wanted with me, but I'd never worried about that with him.

Probably because, deep down inside, I knew he cared about me as a person and not just getting in my pants.

He'd continued the weightlifting once he got back. Though now, he liked to mix his workouts up a bit more, just because he could. So far, he'd gone snowboarding, rafting, hiking... Fucking quite a bit, too. Or so I'd heard. Not that I'd listen to gossip like that deliberately, but sometimes people just said things in public, and it wasn't like I could turn off my ears.

Eli ended the kiss, pulling away as I gave his lip a lingering suck. Then he caught my chin, forcing me to meet his gaze head-on. His eyes were intense. Almost *too* intense.

He was hungry, I realized. And not the kind of hungry you could fix with chicken nuggets.

"Five years," he said, shifting his left leg so that it slid down between mine, spreading my legs wide beneath him. "I sat in that fucking prison cell for five years, and there wasn't a single day that I didn't regret leaving you. Not just leaving the party or getting myself wrapped up in something so much bigger than I could possibly understand at that age, but leaving you. I missed the hell out of that mouth of yours."

"How come you missed me?" I said, the words painful but honest. "I bullied you. Constantly. I couldn't see it through an adult's perspective before. Now I can, and I'm not okay with what I did to you."

Eli pushed his thigh deep between my legs, then started rubbing it back and forth against me. It felt incredible, yet it wasn't quite enough to be satisfying. Just unspeakably distracting. I squirmed beneath him, searching for a spot with just a bit more friction. Eli let out a low laugh, and I realized this wasn't just sex for him.

It was a sensual kind of revenge.

He could torture me for hours like this, bringing me closer to the edge or holding me back, depending on his whims. I tried pushing up and into him with my hips. I just needed a little more—

"So, you want to know why I don't hate you," Eli said, his voice low and husky. I waited, but he took his time, brushing his lips against my cheek. Fuck. I was supposed to be listening to him and owning everything I'd done wrong.

"Okay," I said, trying to focus. It wasn't easy. Every time his thigh drifted over my clit, I sort of lost track of who I was for a moment.

"Hallies Falls is a small town," he said. He'd started kissing softly along my jawline at the same time, which wasn't particularly helpful. Although I hadn't gotten the impression that being helpful was his goal.

"Yeah, I'm fairly sure we all know how small it is," I said, wondering where he was going with this.

"So, when I got here, everyone knew why Gus had taken me in," he said, shifting his hand to my breast. His fingers splayed wide and wrapped around it, giving me a gentle squeeze. "The shit my mom got into was all over the news. I was supposed to be a victim, whether I felt like one or not. The kids at school had to pretend we were friends, even when we hated each other. And all the teachers were so busy feeling sorry for me that none of them bothered to teach me. I was young, but I wasn't stupid. None of them gave a shit about me."

"Wait," I said, not wanting to challenge him, but what he said didn't add up. "You'd already been to first grade when you moved in with Gus. I remember because you were two years older than me, but only one year ahead. They held you back."

"That didn't actually happen," Eli said, pausing to trace my ear lobe with his tongue. "Someone told me to lie about it. Said it would make me fit in better than admitting I'd never been to school. They were wrong."

He gave my ear a sharp nip with his teeth, and I sighed. Couldn't quite decide if that counted as pain or pleasure. Maybe something in the middle.

"So, suddenly, I was in this weird little town where I didn't know anyone. Not even my own uncle. And no matter what I did, everyone treated me like I was weak—"

My snort of laughter cut him off, and he let my boob go long enough to attack my side with a vicious tickle. I screamed, arching under him and begging for mercy. He laughed but let his hand go back to my breast while kissing the side of my neck at the same time. That sent a fresh wave of tingles rushing through me. My hips lifted, my right leg bending and falling to the side.

"So, like I said, they all thought I was some kind of victim, and they treated me that way. Drove me fucking crazy," Eli murmured. "Because I was strong. I'd kept myself and my mom alive. For *years*. And then suddenly I was supposed to turn into a kid again. It was bullshit. All of it. But there was one person who saw through it. You. I was your enemy, and you were out to get me because you knew I was dangerous. Not only that, you saw that being younger was an advantage you could use. Anytime you wanted to, you could've screamed for help, and we both knew people would've taken your word over mine. But you never did."

"Of course not," I said, feeling slightly offended. "That was our only rule. Remember?"

Eli lifted his head, studying my face carefully. I had no idea what he was trying to see—maybe some trace of the little girl I'd been?

"That was the rule, all right. And you never broke it. Not once. That's how I knew I could trust you."

"You trusted me too much," I told him. His fingers let my breast go, only to find it again after sliding his hand up and under my shirt. "I still wish I'd broken it, at least that once. I should've talked to the cops."

"You're really not going to let that go, are you?" he asked, shifting his pelvis so the hard ridge in his jeans could rub back and forth across my hip bone.

"No," I said, determined. Eli started grinding against me, slowly swiveling his hips. Shit. I couldn't think when he did that. Simply wasn't possible. "Let's compromise. We can talk about it after. I don't know how long I can take this. At some point, you're gonna have to fuck me. Sooner rather than later, please."

"I love it when you're all horny," he told me, his voice registering slightly lower than before. At least I wasn't the only one slowly going crazy. "It used to be that I'd get frustrated when I looked back on those years. I needed to learn how to *read*, for fuck's sake. I didn't have time to be a victim. But now, it's our games that I think about the most. They were the only part of my life that made sense."

"Those were fights," I reminded him gently. His fingers found my nipple, holding it lightly. "I never played with you. You broke my teacup."

"Peaches, those were definitely games," he said, and I saw the laughter in his eyes. "My mom and me, we lived on the streets. Sometimes, we'd find an apartment somewhere, but one thing was always the same. There were always predators. Some of them tried to kill us, but a few of them went out of their way to give me the skills I needed to survive in that world. Do you really think that a little girl with a pink foam princess sword could've won against me? I fought other kids for food while our moms got high together."

I shivered, trying to imagine what that might've felt like, but I couldn't. The idea that a child had to fight for food…that was beyond my comprehension. And I'd known he and his mom had been homeless, but that hadn't really meant anything to me back then. To me, *suffering* meant sharing my bedroom. He was right, I'd been naïve as hell.

Too naïve to pity him.

I swallowed, wanting to cry or apologize or *do* something. *Anything.* Except refusing to pity him was the one thing I'd gotten right as a kid. I'd be damned if I'd go weak and fuck it up now, just because I could finally understand the truth.

"What about Lemur?" I asked, trying to lighten the mood. "Was taking him one of those games, too?"

"No." Eli grinned, lifting his hips to reposition himself slightly. "That was something else. That was about the fucking snakes you kept putting in my bed."

I took advantage of his repositioning to slide my hand down between us. Eli was hard as granite, and I felt every inch of his thick, heavy length, despite the fabric separating us.

My fingers tightened around him, and he groaned. Perfect. I wanted to guide the conversation away from the snakes. Talking about them wouldn't end well, for either of us.

"I've never forgotten how much I wanted you that night," I told him softly. "Or how amazing it felt when you touched me."

"I've never forgotten, either," Eli replied. "The good news is that tonight, we're gonna give that another shot. And this time, I don't give a flying fuck if Gus is literally on fire. I'm not leaving you."

Chapter Ten

~Peaches~

Eli's mouth caught mine for another kiss, but this one was different. Deeper. Hungrier. Almost desperate in its intensity. I didn't even notice when his hand drifted down toward my jeans, or when he opened them. The kiss consumed me completely, right up to the instant his finger found my most sensitive spot.

I froze, mesmerized as the digit circled my clit, sending little shockwaves of raw sensation radiating out from my center. At first, there was nothing but perfect pleasure. He'd found exactly the right spot, and now he was utterly focused on working it, every movement slow and steady. Tension started to build within me, along with fresh need.

This was great, but I needed more.

"Faster," I whispered, letting my head fall back. Eli gave a low laugh, but he didn't change what he was doing.

I squirmed, starting to feel frantic. But instead of giving me what I desperately wanted, he pulled away from my clit entirely.

"Eli—" I started to protest, but before I could say more, he plunged his finger all the way into me, hitting my g-spot on the first try. My back arched, and I made a noise halfway between a groan and a scream because whatever he was doing…it worked for me.

Holy hell, it worked.

I'd wanted him to go faster, and now he was. Fast and hard, his fingers plunging just like his dick likely wanted to do. I knew this because my hand was between us, holding him so that every time he moved, I felt just how much he wanted to fuck me.

"I want to see you come first," Eli whispered. As if I had a choice about the sensations ripping through me. That terrible tension was swirling and building with every stroke, and my heart was starting to race.

"That's a great idea," I gasped. I felt like I should remember something, but every time I started to form a coherent thought, that finger of his hit my g-spot again.

Probably something about getting him off, I realized.

Except he'd said he wanted to see *me* get off, which sounded more and more awesome by the second. His hand found a slightly different angle, somehow discovering a way to slide across my clit each and every time. I liked this development.

I liked it a *lot*.

I liked it so much that when he did it again, my toes curled so hard that it hurt, and I started to pant. I was close—really close—and I could feel my orgasm, hovering just out of reach, calling to me. The sound of my heart beating fast filled my ears as every muscle in my body tightened and…*holy shit, was that his thumb touching my*—?

I convulsed once, and then a second time, waves of release smashing through the coiled tension, rocking me in a series of little shocks that left me blinking.

Eli's hand was suddenly on my stomach, rubbing it gently as the last tremors settled. I looked up at him, and he gave me a crooked smile.

"Hell of a bite you got there," he said softly.

"What?"

"You bit my shoulder. Like a vampire. It was hot, but it also kind of hurt."

My eyes focused slowly, and then I saw it. A set of bite marks that were already starting to bruise, right in line with my mouth. I swallowed, trying to remember how that'd happened, and coming up blank.

"I'm sorry?" I said, hoping that was right. Eli's hand slid up, then caught my hair, fisting it as he jerked my head back.

"You're gonna have to make that up to me," he whispered. I tried to answer, but then he kissed me. If the last one had been hungry, this one was starving. He went deep, filling my mouth as he lifted his hips, his hand fumbling with his fly.

I wanted to help, but I couldn't see anything. Suddenly, his jeans were open, and I felt the hard, sleek length of him brush my hand. Then he was settling between my legs, the head of his cock poised at my opening.

Raising his head, Eli pulled away from the kiss. I found myself wanting more and trying to catch him. He caught one of my hands, threading his fingers with mine as he pressed the back of my hand down beside my head.

Then he paused, looking down at me. I couldn't read his expression. In that moment, Eli King was every bit as strange and dangerous as he'd been when I first met him, and he was holding me down.

He could do anything to me, I realized.

Anything at all.

It should've scared me, but instead, it turned me on.

"What's the matter?" I asked. "Are you scared that I'll bite you again?"

Eli slowly shook his head.

"No, you don't scare me."

"Maybe not," I whispered. "But I know what does. You better fuck me right now, or I swear to God, I will fill this whole damned room with snakes while you sleep."

"You are ridiculously fucking crazy," he said. "And now you're mine."

He thrust into me as he said it, filling me so completely that I forgot how to breathe. Then he pulled back and did it again, moving faster with each stroke. Over and over again, he hit that spot inside exactly right, somehow sliding over my clit just enough to qualify as an art form as he did.

This time, I didn't feel a slow build of coiled tension.

I didn't have that luxury.

It was like my wires had gotten crossed, and my body wasn't sure what to do, so I wrapped my legs tightly around his waist and just held on for the ride. I could feel him inside me, pulsing and growing, and I knew he wouldn't last long.

That was okay. I wasn't going to last much longer, either.

I'd just finished the thought when the climax hit, slamming into me as I screamed, convulsing around Eli. It was too much for him. His hips surged into mine one last time, and he jerked as he filled me.

I didn't know how long we stayed like that.

Long enough that I'd stopped shuddering, and my heart rate slowed. We found each other's gazes again, and I watched as a slow change came over his features.

He looked different. Happy.

Smiling.

"So, did you make it ten minutes?" I finally asked. "Because I forgot to hit the stopwatch."

"Don't talk," he said, leaning down to kiss the side of my neck. "I don't want you to ruin it."

Outraged, my hands attacked his sides, and he started laughing. That set me off even more, and then he was tickling me while I tried to attack him with my nails. Then his head hit the wall, and I pressed my attack, rolling him over to climb on top of him.

Not long afterward, I discovered something quite wonderful about Eli King. Apparently, he really was a five-minute man, because that's all it took for him to recover.

Directly after that, I learned something else.

He could keep going for more than ten minutes. Significantly more. So much more, that between the night ending and the next morning beginning, we realized that we absolutely needed to get something to eat.

That's how I found myself on the back of Eli's bike as he tore through the darkness, feeling wild and free in a way I'd never experienced before.

Eventually, Eli pulled off to climb a hill overlooking the valley. There, we sat and ate some snacks we'd gotten at a gas station, laughing and telling stories all the while, refusing to think about anything more than us, right there in that moment. That's when I learned the best thing of all about Eli King.

Seemed he'd always had a fantasy about getting me off while sitting on his Harley, wearing nothing but his belt and a sprinkle of powdered sugar.

I didn't just have a hot biker going down on me in the moonlight that evening.

I had a hot biker going down on me in the moonlight *while I ate mini donuts coated in powdered sugar.*

Life simply did not get any better than that.

The roar of a different motorcycle woke me up early the next morning, just as the sun started to rise.

That'd be Gus, finally coming home from a night of whatever it was he did after the bar closed. I knew this because that'd been his habit ever since I was a little girl. Not every day, but definitely two or three times a week.

I'd loved those mornings.

Mom would still be sleeping, so those were my special times with Gus. He was always in a great mood, too. He'd announce that he wanted waffles, but that he couldn't make them without a helper.

It was my job to watch the waffle iron for when the light turned off so they didn't get burned. Sometimes, I got distracted and missed it. That never bothered Gus, though. He'd just give me a hug and insist that he liked them best when they were extra crispy.

Then we'd sit down and eat together while he told me stories and let me use as much syrup as I wanted. We always finished by putting together a breakfast tray for Mom. Gus had to carry it upstairs, but he'd let me take it into the room to give to her.

Mom loved getting breakfast in bed, sometimes so much that she cried. Tears of happiness, she'd told me, because she had the world's best daughter. Those mornings were some of my favorite childhood memories, pure and beautiful and precious.

Mom's reaction hadn't been tears of happiness, though. I'd figured that out years later once I learned the real reason she left him. The real reason he came home late all those mornings and was in such a good mood.

Eli's arm tightened around my waist, reminding me that I wasn't a little girl anymore. His body spooned mine, our legs tangled together in a delicious echo of what'd happened last night. His solid bulk was comforting, and the gentle rise and fall of his chest reassured me that all was good.

Safe.

Funny how that worked. There wasn't another person on Earth with the power to piss me off like Eli could. Yet when shit got real, we stood together.

Always.

We kept each other's secrets, and while I loved torturing him, I was protective, too. Watching his court case had been like a slow-motion car crash, and his refusal to take my help cut me. Deeply. I'd hated him for it.

I'd also written to him in prison and sent care packages.

Downstairs, the kitchen door thudded as it closed, reminding me that I had unfinished business with Gus. He'd used Eli to save his own ass, something Eli seemed willing to leave in the past.

Very Christian of him, but I was feeling less saintly about the situation.

Eli shifted, rolling onto his back. Moving carefully, I started untangling myself. I hated to leave him, even for a minute. This still felt like some kind of crazy dream that might evaporate if I wasn't careful, but putting things off with Gus would only make it harder in the long run.

I padded to the door, instinctively avoiding the board that creaked. The bedding rustled. I glanced back and saw that Eli had rolled into the warm spot I'd left behind.

His eyes were still closed, and his lips had parted just a bit. He looked so young and innocent...almost sweet. He wasn't innocent, of course. Eli had suffered more as a small child than most people did their entire lives. He'd survived, though. Survived and then sacrificed himself to protect the only family he had left.

Downstairs, I found Gus mixing the waffle batter, whistling a little song to himself. The sound was happy. Cheerful.

"Morning, Peaches," he said, like nothing had changed last night. I suppose that, in his mind, it hadn't. He had no clue that I knew what'd really happened. "Coffee is started. There are fresh strawberries in the fridge if you want some with breakfast."

Walking over to the coffee maker, I pulled out two mugs, filling one for myself and one for Gus. He sprayed the waffle iron, carefully spooning the batter onto the griddle.

"Doesn't look like you slept on the couch last night," he said. "Suppose that means you and Eli—"

"I overheard your meeting at the Starkwood last night," I said, cutting him off. He didn't respond for a moment, just stared down at the waffle iron. "It's time for you to tell me the truth."

He turned to me, his face serious. "Peaches, it's complicated—"

"Is it? Because it seems pretty simple to me. You threw Eli under the bus to save your own ass. You fucked me over, too, but that's kinda minor in comparison. You say it's complicated. Great. You can take as much time as you want to explain it. But I'm not leaving without answers."

"You don't know what you're asking," he said.

"I know Eli won't buy the bar until this talk is over," I countered. "I'm not five years old anymore, okay? I'm an adult. Enough of one to manage your bar for you. So, talk to me."

Pushing off the counter, I held a mug out to him. He took it, and for the first time in my life, I saw his hand shaking. Like an old man's hand, the skin like parchment.

"Let's sit down for this," he said, turning off the waffle iron. I followed him out of the kitchen to the table. We sat down, and I took a sip of my coffee, waiting for him to say something. He didn't, and the silence grew more and more uncomfortable. Finally, he spoke.

"You aren't going to make this easy for me, are you?"

"That's a matter of perspective," I said quietly. "Eli spent five years in prison, covering your ass. Pretty sure this conversation won't take nearly that long."

He swallowed. "I'm afraid you'll never forgive me."

"That's a valid concern," I said quietly. "I can't see myself forgiving you. At least not anytime soon based on what I know right now."

"You never pull your punches, do you?"

"Either you tell her, or I will," Eli said, startling both Gus and me. I looked over at him. He'd pulled on his jeans to come downstairs, but nothing else. His chest was bare, and his hair screamed "*sex.*" I imagined mine did too. Just seeing him made me feel stronger. Safer. Like the two of us could take on the world. He came to stand next to me, resting a hand on my shoulder.

"Okay," Gus said, and I heard the resignation in his voice. "So, it was my birthday party that night. Everyone was down at the Starkwood. I'd spent my afternoon trying to figure out some paperwork. Had a few drinks along the way. Probably a few more than I realized. And, yeah, I know I shouldn't drink and drive. If it makes you feel any better, I haven't since that night."

He paused, taking another sip of coffee.

"So, my doorbell rang. It was Mia Eirwood, carrying her baby. Her husband, Kevin, locked them out of the house. No diaper bag, no cell phone. Nothing. That guy…" Gus shook his head. "That guy was human garbage. And Mia was a sweet little thing. Busted ass working to pay all their bills, all the while Kevin was fucking around on her. He was cooking meth out there, too. Someone needed to do something about him."

"You don't get to be the hero in this story," I said, my voice cold. Gus gave a bark of laughter.

"Oh, I'm aware," he said. "And if I'd been sober, it would have played out different. But that baby was all red from crying, and there was this bruise just starting to form on Mia's neck. I just kept thinking that the next time, he might kill her. Or that lab of his might blow up. Touch off a fire that'd destroy all our homes. Something bad was gonna happen sooner or later. Figured it'd be best if I made him go away. So, I did. I gave her one of those disposable cell phones and told her to call Gage. Said he'd take care of her. Make sure she had protection. That kind of thing."

"Did she know what you were planning?" I asked, remembering the gossip. People had whispered that she'd been sleeping with Eli. That they'd plotted the murder together. But there hadn't been any evidence, and Eli's plea bargain had specifically stipulated that he'd acted alone.

Last I heard, she'd moved to California.

"Naw, she was just a kid," Gus said. "Clueless. So, I grabbed my gun and took the pickup over to his place. Figured I'd kill him and then stash the body somewhere before hitting the party."

Gus's voice was so casual as he talked about stashing a body. Scary casual, as if he were talking about a bag of recyclables. Not a person. Eli's hand tightened on my shoulder, reminding me that I wasn't alone.

"I already told you I was drunk," Gus continued. His eyes were fixed on the wall across from him. Maybe a part of him had to pretend that he was alone to say these things out loud.

"Wasn't thinking it through, obviously. Everything went just fine until I ran the truck off the road. Hit my head pretty good in the process, which didn't help. Couldn't get the truck out of the ditch, so I called Gage. He got Eli and sent him and Pipes to deal with it. It's hard to remember the exact order of everything."

"Gus was drunk," Eli said flatly. "And he definitely had a concussion. We used Pipes' big diesel to pull the truck out of the ditch. I sent Pipes and Gus back to the party—wanted to establish at least a partial alibi—and then I drove the pickup back to the house. Parked it in the shed. The plan was for me to ride Gus's Harley back to the bar. I'd just pulled out of the driveway when a sheriff's deputy pulled me over."

"I was an idiot," Gus said quietly. "About everything. And sloppy. Didn't even notice an extra car in the Eirwood's driveway. There was someone inside the house besides just Kevin. Whoever it was saw the whole thing. Apparently, they ransacked the house afterward. About an hour later, someone made an anonymous call to the cops to report what'd happened. You probably remember that part from the appeal."

"I do remember it," I said quietly. "Because the sheriff's deputy had no reason to pull Eli over. He just assumed he was involved because he's a biker."

"Exactly," said Eli. "But we didn't know that until a lot later."

"People are too damned prejudiced," Gus muttered. I shot him a dirty look.

"You actually committed this particular crime, Gus," I reminded him. "And then Eli went to prison for it. Not you."

Eli straightened and then stepped around the table to sit down facing me. I reached my hand out toward him, and he took it.

"I made a choice," Eli said quietly. "Washington has a three strikes law, and Gus already had two. They'd have put him away for life. Worst case, we knew I'd still be eligible for parole."

"The lawyers said the appeal was strong," Gus added defensively. "The deputy claimed that he'd stopped Eli based on that 911 call, but they couldn't produce a witness or a recording. Sure as shit didn't have a warrant. I knew we'd get Eli out eventually."

"And what about the Reapers?" I asked. "What did they think?"

"It doesn't matter," Eli told me. "None of it. I'm out of prison, and it's all over. They never tied Gus to the crime at all."

"Gage said it was bullshit," Gus said, his voice haunted. "They wanted to fight it all the way. Eli was more worried about protecting me than he was about himself. He figured that if your alibi accounted for him, then they'd start looking at me. You were part of it, too."

That caught me off guard. "What?"

"Gus is talking out of his ass," Eli said, shooting him a nasty look.

"He didn't want you to lose me," Gus said, ignoring Eli. "He'd already watched you lose me once. Didn't want to see it again. So, he took the bullet and pleaded out. Lawyers helped him with that part…the whole thing was a setup, 'cause they were already planning the appeal."

I couldn't breathe, trying to comprehend what Gus had just told me.

"Eli?" I finally asked, still trying to wrap my head around it. "Is that true?"

He shrugged, glaring at Gus. "It was a small factor. Not the only, though. So, don't get too full of yourself. If it makes you feel better, I had plenty of time to think things over while I was locked up. I should've fought from the beginning and let it play out naturally. For what it's worth, Gus didn't talk to me before offering to sell you the bar. He already knew my feelings on the subject. I was totally against it, and I still am. It's too fucking dangerous."

"So, it's too dangerous for me but okay for you?"

"I'm a member of the club," Eli said. "I took on that risk when I joined. You're a civilian."

"But why should *either* of us have to be at risk?" I demanded. "Why can't one of us just buy the Starkwood and run it? No Reapers, no danger, just good food and cold beer!"

"Because the Reapers own half the business," Gus said quietly.

That threw me.

"No, they don't," I said. "You do. James looked up the property values and the liquor license and… Oh, shit. You mean they own it secretly. Like the Mafia or something?"

"I inherited the bar," Gus said. "You knew that. Well, I didn't get it free and clear. It came with a lot of debt. Eventually, I wanted to buy a house, but I couldn't get a loan from a bank. So, I asked the Reapers if they'd be willing to buy a stake in the business. They said yes. There aren't any records, of course, but Eli has known about it for years."

"So you're saying the Reapers Motorcycle Club owns half the bar you wanted me to buy from you," I said slowly. "Were you planning to tell me this before or after I signed the papers?"

"I'd have told you before," Gus said. His eyes had reddened, the surface shiny with tears. For an instant, I felt sorry for him. Then I remembered all the times my mom had cried when I brought a tray of waffles to her in bed.

I wanted to believe that he'd have been honest with me before it was too late.

"You're an incredibly selfish person," I said, pushing my chair back as I stood. "I don't even know what to say to you. Other people aren't just tissues to be used and thrown away when they get inconvenient, Gus. I can't believe I used to wish you were my dad."

Turning my back on him, I walked toward the stairs, trying to think. Obviously, I couldn't buy the bar. But Eli shouldn't buy it, either. I knew the club was into illegal stuff. I wasn't a total idiot. But what Gus had described…that was serious shit. They had to be laundering money or something.

The thought stopped me in my tracks.

I'd been doing the Starkwood books for two years. Obviously, not the real books, but I'd seen enough that it'd been confusing at times. Now, everything made so much more sense. This was horrible. But it might also be an opportunity.

"Eli, can I talk to you upstairs?"

* * * *

~Eli~

I wasn't quite sure what to expect when I followed Peaches upstairs.

I'd seen her angry plenty of times throughout the years. Hell, she was mad around me more often than not, usually because I provoked her, which was definitely my second favorite way to spend time with her.

I'd never seen Peaches like this, though.

She wasn't screaming or throwing things. There was no fire in her eyes. If anything, she seemed to be concentrating really hard. Like she had an idea, which was a turn of events that rarely ended well for me. My dick gave an optimistic twitch as she sat down on the bed. The room still smelled like sex, for fuck's sake, but I had no illusions.

Whatever she wanted to talk about didn't involve me getting laid. So, when she leaned back against the wall, looking toward the door, I leaned back next to her.

"So this whole time, you were only going to buy half the bar," she said slowly. "And you always knew that was the deal."

"Yup. I've known it since I turned eighteen. The Reapers have been silent partners since before we were born."

"And you're okay with that?" she asked, turning to look at me.

"It is what it is," I said. "You're not stupid. You know the Reapers are into all kinds of things. Gus and I are both part of that. I chose this life, and I'm at peace with what it means."

"And the Reapers had nothing to do with you serving time? They didn't ask you to do that?"

"No, they didn't," I said. "This wasn't about the club at all. They paid for my lawyer—we have a fund for that—and they bought a pig to roast at the party when I got out. But shooting that guy? That was Gus, all by himself. He called us for help, and we answered because that's what we do."

"He may not always be right, but he's always your brother..." she said, the words trailing off. I nodded, and we both fell silent again. Her hand slipped down, catching mine. I raised it to my mouth, kissing her fingers.

"So, I have this thought," Peaches said, breaking the silence.

"I'm listening."

"What if we bought the bar together?" she asked. "If we put our money together, we'd have enough to buy all of them out. Last night, you said you wanted to be partners with me. That it didn't matter whose name was on the deed. I thought you were full of shit, but that's the kind of partnership the Reapers have with Gus already, isn't it?"

"Well, that wasn't exactly what I was thinking," I admitted.

Peaches laughed.

"You were thinking more about me putting in my time and energy there the same way I would if I owned a stake. You'd let me make decisions, and we'd be like partners, except your name would be on the deed, and you'd have the power to fire me."

"When you put it like that, it sounds bad," I admitted. She offered me her sweetest smile, and suddenly, all I could think about were those lips of hers wrapped around my cock.

"It *is* bad," she said. "But I have a different idea. One that could work for both of us. What if I buy out Gus, and you buy out the Reapers? That way, you're the silent partner, and unlike me, you'd actually have the force to assert your rights if I decided to cheat you."

I stilled, almost startled by how obvious it was.

"Do you think we could do it?" I asked her. "Let's assume that the financing works, and the Reapers are on board—and I'm thinking I could make that happen—do you really think you and I could be equal partners in something like that? Without killing each other?"

"Have we killed each other yet?" she asked, her voice softening. She tugged her hand free from mine and then dropped it to my inner thigh, rubbing it back and forth. My dick took notice, and I felt my balls clench. Then her fingers drifted up, cupping me and fondling me through my jeans.

"You came close last night," I said, trying to follow the conversation. Hard to concentrate, given what she was doing. Peaches touched her lips to mine, just the hint of a teasing kiss. Then she pulled away.

"You're my best friend, Eli. I'm attracted to you, and I definitely like having sex with you. I've spent hundreds—maybe thousands—of hours thinking up new ways to make your life a living hell, yet you still go out of your way to run into me. You like being with me as much as I like being with you."

"I'd rather be in you," I said. In a flash, she jerked her hand away from my dick to punch my shoulder. She hit hard, too. Not hard enough to hurt me for real, but she wasn't playing around, either.

"God, you're an asshole. I'm trying to have a serious talk here!"

"You know, it turns me on when you're mad enough to call me names," I said, which was true. Her eyes had reclaimed their sparkle, and her cheeks were flushed.

"You're like a two-year-old."

"And yet you keep coming back for more," I pointed out. "That's what you just said, right?"

Peaches opened her mouth to argue, then snapped it shut again. She closed her eyes and took a deep breath. When she opened them again, her face was serious.

"Are you going to buy the bar with me or not?"

It was a great question. A complicated one, too. Not because I didn't think we could work together. I *knew* we could work together. But there was more at stake here than the business.

"Question for you," I said, catching her hand again. "We've known each other for most of our lives. If we buy the bar together, we're stuck with each other. Maybe not forever, but for a long time."

"I know."

"I can't run a business with you and watch you fuck some other guy, let alone marry him or carry his babies. I've always known you'll settle down someday, and I'm not lying when I say I wish you the best in life. But once you marry someone else, I don't want to be trapped in a business partnership with you. That's my definition of hell."

Her eyes widened, and she swallowed. "So, what's your question?"

I paused, the words on the tip of my tongue. Once I said them out loud, everything would change. Either she'd be with me or she wouldn't.

Fuck it.

"If we're going to buy the Starkwood together, we should get married."

"Eli—"

"Hear me out, first, okay? I just think that—"

"*Eli*—"

"Just listen to me. Then—"

"Eli, I'm trying to—"

"Christ, Peaches. Just give me—"

"Shut the fuck up!" she burst out, and I could hear the laughter in her voice. "I keep trying to say yes, but you're so in love with the sound of your own damned voice that you can't even—"

My hand caught the back of her head, ending the argument with a kiss. Her arms came around me, pulling me down over her body as she collapsed backward onto the bed.

Time seemed to freeze in that instant, marking the spot where my life transitioned from before to after. Was this really happening?

"Hey!" Peaches said, snapping her fingers at me. "Pay attention."

"What?"

"I asked if you were serious about me carrying babies," she said. "But you were zoned out or something. Which isn't exactly flattering, considering we're in the middle of something physical here."

"Um, probably," I told her. "I mean, I'd like to have kids someday."

"That's good," she said, biting her lip. "Because we didn't use any condoms last night, and I just realized that I forgot to refill my prescription this month."

I blinked, growing very still. "So, you could be pregnant...?"

"Theoretically," she said. "I mean, people have sex all the time without getting knocked up. But it's nice to know you wouldn't be upset. At the very least, it seemed like something I should mention before we have sex again. Because that's the direction this is heading, right?"

"Yeah, that was the plan," I said. "Are you okay with it?"

Her eyes turned thoughtful, and then she started to nod slowly. "I think I am. We should do this, Eli."

"What? Fuck? Buy the bar? Get married?"

"All of it. I want to do all of it."

"Can we start with the fucking?" I asked.

"I think that can be arranged."

Epilogue

One year later

~Peaches~

"Okay, you can look now," Mom said. "What do you think?"

I opened my eyes, gasping at my reflection in the half-circle of mirrors strategically surrounding my little platform. I still looked like me, of course—same dark hair, although it'd gotten thicker. Same face, complete with a random zit on the chin. Same waistline I'd had when Eli and I had finally admitted how we felt about each other.

Hadn't seen *that* for a while.

Kinda nice to realize it still existed, even if it took a corset to coax it out.

My boobs were another story. They'd always been generous, and they'd gotten more so with a side of backache once the babies arrived. I'd come to accept this new reality, even if I wasn't totally comfortable with it. Usually, I just threw on a big T-shirt and called it good.

This dress was a hell of a lot more tailored than a T-shirt, though. I took a deep breath—well, as deep as I could—watching first with awe and then something closer to fear as my chest expanded upward and outward from the dress, yet somehow didn't break free in an explosion of overpriced fabric.

"Do you have any idea how much money you could make stripping right now?" Megan asked.

"Not enough to cover daycare for twins," I told her, turning to the side to study my profile. Holy shit, was that really me in the mirror? Nipped-in tummy, massive rack. Hips that flared out just the right amount, all draped in a classic white mermaid dress so perfect a princess could've worn it.

"Do you see that?" I asked. "Or am I hallucinating?"

"See what?" Mom asked.

"My waist," I said, feeling almost giddy.

"Of course, I can see your waist," she said. "Don't tell me you aren't happy with your figure, Peaches, because you look amazing. I know you're frustrated that you haven't lost all the weight yet. But that's not realistic. Women are *supposed* to have some extra while they're nursing. It took a million years of evolution to create those curves of yours, and you should be proud of them."

I laughed, shaking my head.

"I'm not upset," I told her. "I'm just excited to see it again. When the salesperson brought that corset into the changing room, I thought she was crazy. I'm a believer now."

"Foundation garments are critical," said the sales associate, smiling at me.

"What about her boobs?" asked Randi, one of my friends. We'd grown up together, but we'd only gotten really close over the last couple of years. "I think it's amazing they haven't popped out yet, but that fabric looks really delicate. Are you sure it'll hold?"

"This is where strategic taping comes in," the associate said, her voice confident. "It may look like her décolletage is insecure, but she could jump on a trampoline if she wanted to. We take these things very seriously."

I gave a little hop, watching as my girls flew up and then came in for a safe landing.

"We'll take it," Mom announced. "All of it. And throw in some extra tape, too."

"It's too much," I said, shaking my head. "Things are tight enough already financially, and we're still getting hospital bills. It's really gorgeous, but I can't justify it. What about that other one? The one on sale?"

Megan and Randi exchanged dark looks, and the sales associate literally flinched—a response reflected back to me in all six mirrors.

"James and I will be paying for the dress," Mom said.

"Mom—"

"He said if you argued, I should threaten to tell you what we did in bed last night. And then again this morning. I don't want to give out any spoilers, but it involved a new kind of lube. Originally developed at NASA, according to James. You can use it for anything, but I really like it for—"

My vision narrowed, turning black around the edges as I swayed. The sales lady and Randi each caught one of my arms, easing me down.

"Are you all right?" Randi asked. I shook my head.

"No," I said, shuddering.

"Still want to argue about who's paying for the dress?" Mom asked.

I looked up at her, wondering how such a sweet-looking woman could be so sadistic.

"Thank you very much for your generous gift."

Two hours later, I walked through the door of the Starkwood Saloon in full wedding hair and makeup. It was only a test run, but seeing my sleep-deprived eyes without black circles was almost as good as discovering I still had a waist.

Several of our regulars were already there for the afternoon, all of them asking about the wedding plans as I passed through. I answered as quickly as possible, eager to see my babies. The office door stood open a few inches, which meant they weren't asleep. They weren't crying, either. Things must've gone well.

"Eli, you won't believe—" The words died as I stepped into the room. "I didn't realize Gus was here."

Eli sat on the couch, cradling Lynette as he gave her a bottle. Next to him was Gus, holding my son, Augie. Gus looked up at me, his face full of wonder.

"I can't believe how tiny they are," he said. "You did a hell of a job, Peaches."

"I thought you were still in Mexico," I said slowly. "You should've let us know you'd be in town."

"So you could avoid me?" he asked. I considered lying, but decided the truth was better.

"Yes."

I shot a dirty look at Eli, which he pretended not to notice. We'd have words about this little ambush later.

"Gus needs to talk to you about something."

"I'm not sure we have anything to talk about."

"I'm pretty sure you do," Eli said, leaning forward a little to balance himself before standing up from the couch. "Lynette and I are gonna go check on the bar."

He gave me a quick kiss on the cheek as he brushed past, which I allowed because I looked particularly good at the moment. Best for him to be fully aware of what he was missing when he didn't get laid tonight.

I closed the door, then walked over to the couch. Gus looked old, especially next to the baby. I wanted to rip Augie out of his arms, but my boy was asleep. Eli and I had a second rule now—never wake a sleeping baby. And it came with built-in consequences.

"You had something you wanted to say?" I asked.

The old man nodded.

"I love you," he said.

"Great," I told him. "Glad we clarified that. You can leave now."

"I'm sorry I wasn't a better man," he added. "I'm really proud of you, Peaches."

Silence fell between us, broken only by a tiny baby snore.

"You know I love you, too," I told Gus.

"You always have. I took that for granted for a long time. I won't do that ever again."

His words pulled at my heart, reminding me of how much faith I'd put in him. How much I'd been willing to overlook. A part of me wanted to fall into his arms and cry because he'd always been my safe place.

"I had you on a hell of a pedestal," I admitted. "I should've seen it earlier."

"That I'm a selfish bastard?" he asked, quirking his mouth.

"Something like that."

"I can't go back and change things, baby girl," he said quietly. "But I'd sure like the chance to prove I'm a changed man now."

"Actions speak louder than words," I said. Augie snorted, stirring in Gus's arms. We both watched as little hand stretched open, then relaxed again as he drifted back to sleep.

"I understand," Gus said. "I know it won't happen overnight. But sooner or later—if you give me a chance—it'll happen. You'll see that I've changed."

"Did you have anything else you wanted to talk about?" I said, suddenly uncomfortable. "I'm sure you have things to do. Wouldn't want to keep you."

"I have a present for you," he said, nodding toward a large manila envelope sitting on the desk. "You and the babies. Go ahead and open it. Eli already knows about it."

"Nice of you guys to wait for me…"

"I needed to run it by him," Gus explained. "Make sure he understood."

I shot him a look, then picked up the envelope. A sheaf of papers slid out, and I skimmed the one on top. Letterhead from a lawyer's office. Was I reading it wrong? Because it looked like...

"It's the house," Gus said. "I'm giving it to you."

I blinked. "You're giving me and Eli the house?"

"No," he said. "I'm giving *you* the house. I'm hoping you and Eli will decide to live there, but that's your decision to make. Not mine."

"Why?" I asked, stunned. "This isn't about money, Gus. You can't buy me off with a house. I can't accept this."

"Don't accept it for yourself. Accept it for your babies. You can sell it someday, maybe pay for their college."

"I have absolutely no clue what to say," I admitted. "This feels wrong. Weird. What the fuck, Gus?"

"I want you to have it because I made a promise to your mother," he said. "When she left me."

"What was that?"

"That if she let me stay in your life, I'd never hurt you. And then I broke that promise. Like you said, actions speak louder than words. I can't give her the security or peace of mind that I took from her all those years ago. But I can give it to you, and her grandchildren. This is my apology."

My eyes watered, and I blinked furiously, trying not to cry. "Fuck you, Gus. I can't believe I'm falling for your shit again."

"So you'll take the house?"

I reached for a tissue from the box on the desk, blotting my eyes carefully, then nodded.

"I'll take it. But I'm still pissed at you for a lot of reasons. Including fucking up my makeup when I finally look decent for the first time in months."

A slow smile spread across his face, and Gus looked ten years younger. "Thank you, baby."

"Don't read too much into it," I snapped. "I'm not asking you to walk me down the aisle."

"I know."

The door opened.

"All good in here?" Eli asked, pitching his voice low as he stepped inside. "Lynette fell asleep."

"Not yet," I replied. "But it will be. Kids will have to share a bedroom, though. Sooner or later, we'll have to tell them we did the same thing. Could get weird."

"Shit," said Gus. "I hadn't thought of that."

"It'll be fine," Eli told me. "We'll just need to make sure they're both scared of snakes. Mutually assured destruction."

"Is that how it works?" I asked.

"It's always worked for us," he replied. "Hey, Gus?"

"Yeah?"

"Why don't you take Augie for a little walk so I can have some alone time—well, partial alone time—with his mama."

"Too soon," I told him. "I'm still pissed at you for setting up an ambush."

Eli gave me a look. "Seriously?"

I decided to let him off the hook. "No, I'm not pissed at you. But I'm not ready to let him take Augie for walks around the bar yet, either."

"That's good with me," Gus said, clearing his throat. "Because I think this kid needs to be changed. That's a little outside my area of expertise."

"I got it," Eli said.

"I can do it," I told him. "You watched him all afternoon."

"Yeah, but he might spray you and ruin your makeup. That'll put you in a bad mood, which could fuck up my plan to get laid tonight."

"So you think you're getting laid tonight?" I asked, catching a strand of my hair, then twisting it around my finger.

"Pretty sure of it," Eli said.

"Why's that?"

"Because I have something you want."

"I'm still in the room," Gus said. "Just in case you've forgotten."

"Shut up, Gus," I said, watching as Eli carefully set Lynette down in her little bassinet. He walked over to the battered old file cabinet that'd been in the office for years, opened the bottom drawer, and pulled out a brown paper bag. It looked old, and I could see dust in the creases.

"I meant to give you this years ago," Eli said. "But I kept putting it off, and then I forgot about it. When Gus talked to me about giving you the house, it came back to me."

"I had no clue it was in his closet," Gus said, clearing his throat. "He only told me this morning."

I frowned as Eli handed me the bag. The paper was stiff, but after a few seconds, I managed to open it. What was that? It almost looked like...

"No way," I said, pulling out a little stuffed animal. He looked exactly the same...well, mostly the same, anyway. Probably better not to think about his tail. "It's Lemur. I thought you buried him out in the woods!"

"I know," Eli said, clearing his throat. "I always planned to give him back. I really did. The tail, too. That was supposed to be a joke, but then you freaked out, and I realized how bad I fucked up."

"Why didn't you just tell me?" I asked. "I missed him so much, Eli."

He shrugged. "Maybe holding onto him was an excuse."

"To do what? Fight with me?"

"Fighting was better than nothing," Eli said. "In a weird way, Lemur tied us together. Except we've got kids now, and we're getting married. Pretty sure I can fight with you anytime I want at this point."

I hugged Lemur close, closing my eyes to savor the feel of his tiny body in my arms. It wasn't the same, though. He smelled weird. And his fur wasn't as soft as I remembered. Nowhere near as soft as Lynette's and Augie's hair.

"I'll take him now," Eli said to Gus. I opened my eyes to watch them—the two most important men in my life, carefully transferring my son from one set of hands to the next, and something inside me shifted.

It took a second to realize what it was.

My anger.

It was gone.

Gus had been right. He'd said it would happen, and it had. I'd forgiven him. It didn't change what'd happened in the past, and I had no clue how things would be in the future. But for the first time since I was five years old, everything was right again.

I gave Lemur another hug, then set him down on the couch. Lynette had started to wake up, and she needed me a lot more than Lemur did. Someday, she'd be big enough to have tea parties on the porch, I realized.

My porch.

I couldn't wait.

* * * *

Also from 1001 Dark Nights and Joanna Wylde, discover *Shade's Lady* and *Rome's Chance*.

Sign up for the 1001 Dark Nights Newsletter
and be entered to win a Tiffany Key necklace.

There's a contest every month!

Go to www.1001DarkNights.com to subscribe.

**As a bonus, all subscribers can download
FIVE FREE exclusive books!**

QUIET MAN by Kristen Ashley
A Dream Man Novella

ABANDON by Rachel Van Dyken
A Seaside Pictures Novella

THE OPEN DOOR by Laurelin Paige
A Found Duet Novella

CLOSER by Kylie Scott
A Stage Dive Novella

SOMETHING JUST LIKE THIS by Jennifer Probst
A Stay Novella

BLOOD NIGHT by Heather Graham
A Krewe of Hunters Novella

TWIST OF FATE by Jill Shalvis
A Heartbreaker Bay Novella

MORE THAN PLEASURE YOU by Shayla Black
A More Than Words Novella

WONDER WITH ME by Kristen Proby
A With Me In Seattle Novella

THE DARKEST ASSASSIN by Gena Showalter
A Lords of the Underworld Novella

Also from 1001 Dark Nights:
DAMIEN by J. Kenner

Discover 1001 Dark Nights

Go to www.1001DarkNights.com for more information.

COLLECTION ONE
FOREVER WICKED by Shayla Black
CRIMSON TWILIGHT by Heather Graham
CAPTURED IN SURRENDER by Liliana Hart
SILENT BITE: A SCANGUARDS WEDDING by Tina Folsom
DUNGEON GAMES by Lexi Blake
AZAGOTH by Larissa Ione
NEED YOU NOW by Lisa Renee Jones
SHOW ME, BABY by Cherise Sinclair
ROPED IN by Lorelei James
TEMPTED BY MIDNIGHT by Lara Adrian
THE FLAME by Christopher Rice
CARESS OF DARKNESS by Julie Kenner

COLLECTION TWO
WICKED WOLF by Carrie Ann Ryan
WHEN IRISH EYES ARE HAUNTING by Heather Graham
EASY WITH YOU by Kristen Proby
MASTER OF FREEDOM by Cherise Sinclair
CARESS OF PLEASURE by Julie Kenner
ADORED by Lexi Blake
HADES by Larissa Ione
RAVAGED by Elisabeth Naughton
DREAM OF YOU by Jennifer L. Armentrout
STRIPPED DOWN by Lorelei James
RAGE/KILLIAN by Alexandra Ivy/Laura Wright
DRAGON KING by Donna Grant
PURE WICKED by Shayla Black
HARD AS STEEL by Laura Kaye
STROKE OF MIDNIGHT by Lara Adrian
ALL HALLOWS EVE by Heather Graham
KISS THE FLAME by Christopher Rice
DARING HER LOVE by Melissa Foster
TEASED by Rebecca Zanetti
THE PROMISE OF SURRENDER by Liliana Hart

DIRTY FILTHY FIX by Laurelin Paige
THE BED MATE by Kendall Ryan
NIGHT GAMES by CD Reiss
NO RESERVATIONS by Kristen Proby
DAWN OF SURRENDER by Liliana Hart

COLLECTION FIVE
BLAZE ERUPTING by Rebecca Zanetti
ROUGH RIDE by Kristen Ashley
HAWKYN by Larissa Ione
RIDE DIRTY by Laura Kaye
ROME'S CHANCE by Joanna Wylde
THE MARRIAGE ARRANGEMENT by Jennifer Probst
SURRENDER by Elisabeth Naughton
INKED NIGHTS by Carrie Ann Ryan
ENVY by Rachel Van Dyken
PROTECTED by Lexi Blake
THE PRINCE by Jennifer L. Armentrout
PLEASE ME by J. Kenner
WOUND TIGHT by Lorelei James
STRONG by Kylie Scott
DRAGON NIGHT by Donna Grant
TEMPTING BROOKE by Kristen Proby
HAUNTED BE THE HOLIDAYS by Heather Graham
CONTROL by K. Bromberg
HUNKY HEARTBREAKER by Kendall Ryan
THE DARKEST CAPTIVE by Gena Showalter

Also from 1001 Dark Nights:

TAME ME by J. Kenner
THE SURRENDER GATE By Christopher Rice
SERVICING THE TARGET By Cherise Sinclair
TEMPT ME by J. Kenner

About Joanna Wylde

Joanna Wylde started her writing career in journalism, working in two daily newspapers as both a reporter and editor. Her career has included many different jobs, from managing a homeless shelter to running her own freelance writing business, where she took on projects ranging from fundraising to ghostwriting for academics. During 2012 she got her first Kindle reader as a gift and discovered the indie writing revolution taking place online. Not long afterward she started cutting back her client list to work on Reaper's Property, her breakout book. It was published in January 2013, marking the beginning of a new career writing fiction.

Joanna lives in the mountains of northern Idaho with her family.

Discover More Joanna Wylde

Shade's Lady: A Reapers MC Novella
By Joanna Wylde

Looking back, none of this would've happened if I hadn't dropped my phone in the toilet. I mean, I could've walked away from him if I'd had it with me.

Or maybe not.

Maybe it was all over the first time he saw me, and he would've found another way. Probably—if there's one thing I've learned, it's that Shade always gets what he wants, and apparently he wanted me.

Right from the first.

* * * *

Rome's Chance: A Reapers MC Novella
By Joanna Wylde

Rome McGuire knew he was in trouble the first time he saw her.

She was sweet and pretty and just about perfect in every way. She was also too young and innocent for the Reapers Motorcycle Club. He did the right thing and walked away.

The second time, he couldn't resist tasting her.

Gorgeous and smart, fun and full of wonder, she jumped on his bike and would've followed him anywhere. Still, she deserved a shot at happiness somewhere bigger and better than a town like Hallies Falls. Walking away wasn't so easy that time, but her family needed her and he had a job to do.

When she came around a third time, he'd had enough. Randi Whittaker had been given two chances to escape, and now it was time for Rome to take his.

This time, the only way Randi would be leaving Hallies Falls was on the back of Rome's bike.

On behalf of 1001 Dark Nights,

Liz Berry and M.J. Rose would like to thank ~

Steve Berry
Doug Scofield
Kim Guidroz
Jillian Stein
InkSlinger PR
Dan Slater
Asha Hossain
Chris Graham
Chelle Olson
Kasi Alexander
Jessica Johns
Dylan Stockton
Richard Blake
and Simon Lipskar